BAD SEED

BAD

THE FEMINIST PRESS
AT THE CITY UNIVERSITY OF NEW YORK
NEW YORK CITY

SEED

STORIES

GABRIEL CARLE

Translated from the Spanish by Heather Houde

Published in 2024 by the Feminist Press
at the City University of New York
The Graduate Center
365 Fifth Avenue, Suite 5406
New York, NY 10016

feministpress.org

First Feminist Press edition 2024

Mala Leche was originally published in Spanish in Puerto Rico by Ediciones Alayubia in 2018. The stories "Devilwork" and "Helium" were written in English by José Gabriel Figueroa Carle and appear here for the first time.

"In Heat" appeared in *The Common*, issue 24, in October 2022.

"Luisito" appeared in *Southwest Review*,
volume 107, issue 3, in October 2022.

This book is made possible by the New York State
Council on the Arts with the support of the
Office of the Governor and the New York State Legislature.

This book was published with financial support
from the Jerome Foundation.

First printing May 2024

Cover design by Dana Li
Text design by Drew Stevens

Library of Congress Cataloging-in-Publication Data is available for this title.
ISBN 978-1-55861-320-1

PRINTED IN THE UNITED STATES OF AMERICA

A Yeya, a Ma, a Pa

Contents

In Heat

It's the last day of school and I get home with butterflies in my stomach. My mouth already tastes like summer, like heat outside and AC inside, like the darkness of my cave, like cloister and crypt. I turn on the TV and change the channel, change the channel, one to the next, checking the lineup that will feed my hunger for the rest of the night, the rest of the weekend, the rest of summer break.

I'm used to my mom being home most days, holed up with her romance novels, because she doesn't have any special-ed kids to teach at her school. I'm used to my grandfather at his desk, in the armchair in front of the television, in the living room glued to the computer for hours playing online poker, acting like the least grown-up old man I know. I'm used to my grandmother telling me to shut off the AC at ten o'clock every morning, yelling at me to make my bed, or pick up my dishes, or put away the clothes on the floor—picking a fight with me because all I do is watch TV in my room, play Wii, look for ungodly things on the internet, which I take care to do at four in the morning when everyone is asleep except for me, with my left hand on my dick, my right on the mouse, and the cockroaches scurrying up the walls.

I get up every day at eight in the morning to glue myself to Lifetime and watch *The Golden Girls*, followed by two episodes of *Frasier*, followed by two hours of *The Nanny*, followed by two more episodes of *The Golden Girls*, followed by two episodes of *Desperate Housewives*, followed by two hours of *Grey's Anatomy*. The daily spiral: the same lineup, the same lines, and the same episodes since I discovered channel 42 (now channel 25) in the fourth grade and, thanks to closed-captioning, found the perfect way to practice my English, so I could perfect my sarcasm, and wait for the laugh track, so I could learn to be a destructive-rebel-anarchist teen who cries too much and who locks himself in the bathroom every night at seven p.m. to shower and scrub off his filth before disappearing into the steam.

In the afternoons the sun blares down and the grackles scream their mating calls. I melt into bed with a fan aimed at my face, with my grandmother jotting down recipes from Food Network, my grandfather playing solitaire on the computer, and my mom getting home from the movies exhausted (I didn't want to go with her, didn't want to get out of bed, didn't want to brush my teeth) and locking herself in her room to pick up where she left off with whatever romance novel. I imagine myself surrounded by Brazilian dicks and African American dicks and Sean Cody models fucking bareback with little beads of sweat sliding down the hair on their orifices like pearls.

I can't get on the computer right now, can't get any relief, there are too many witnesses. My hand tightens around the remote control and I listen for changes in my periphery, flicking randomly, channels in English, Spanish, English, English, English, Spanish, English, English, Uruguayan Spanish, Spanish Spanish, Argentine Spanish, British English, and I land on the History Channel, falling into a new documentary, *The Universe*, and I discover the universe, the planet, the Caribbean, the island, San Juan, my bedroom, through the TV static, and the waves bounce off the worn cement walls.

Night comes and I enter prime-time territory: *Family Guy*, *American Dad*, *The Simpsons*, *South Park*, *Robot Chicken*, *Whose Line Is It Anyway?*, UFC (if it's Tuesday or Thursday or Friday), and I jerk off to the wrestlers throwing each other to the ground in front of a bloodthirsty crowd. I land on Disney, horror of horrors. Why the fuck am I still watching this channel? Instantly erasing all memory of Lizzie McGuire and Raven-Symoné and Kim Possible, I don't have time for that childishness—it's time to take advantage of the tropical silence, of my family's deep, air-conditioned sleep. I sneak into the living room and hold my shirt between my teeth, drenching it with saliva, making sure not to get a drop of cum on it, so all of those shining white pearls land on my stomach and I can feel the true heat of adolescence on my skin. They've never caught me at this hour: I erase the stains, erase the history, erase every horny trace. I heat up some Tyson nuggets in the toaster oven, turn on the TV, and it's still Toonami at four, five, six in the morning. The static fills the space between my thoughts.

Another Saturday, Sunday, Monday night emptying the freezer and filling my mind with dubbed-over Japanese for a Caribbean audience that pays an exorbitant amount of money for the few channels that come through. No one from school calls to invite me over, and anyway, why would I want to go? If I went out I'd miss the new Lifetime movie, or the new Comedy Central roast, or the new debut on FX, or whatever new gay show Bravo is premiering. Next summer I'll get a job. Next month I'll do my summer reading. Next week I'll crawl out of my hole. Tomorrow I'll wash off the stains.

During the summer I get used to dense humidity in my bones, vapor dripping down the walls, the dirty walls of my dirty room, and my mirror covered with the remains of popped pimples and semen that explode out of my reach. Days pass, weeks pass, but the television is eternal, the shows stay the same, the fourth of July passes and the barrage of familial visits to Puerto Rico come to pass: my aunt from Denver comes with her husband and my four-year-old cousin to stay in Isla Verde, then my uncle comes from Orlando with my two cousins to stay with my aunt in Isla Verde, then my other uncle comes from his apartment in Chelsea to take pictures of the facade of a family that makes the effort to get together even if it's just once a year, pictures of daughters that call every Sunday and sons that call once every couple weeks, if that. I bought myself *Zelda: Twilight Princess* last week and now spend my hours trying to beat the goddamn game. It expands and becomes infinite—infinite pastures that open wider and wider and wider, into new worlds and new dimensions I can't control, I can't control, I can't pull myself away from the TV, I don't want to go to the beach, I don't want any barbecue, I don't want to hand over the remote control, I don't want anyone to bother me, ever. Fuck, why don't my cousins go play volleyball or something? They won't leave me alone and I'm so close to beating this level, soon I'll be battling Ganondorf and I'm going to fuck him up, I'm going to fuck him up, Link is going to fuck him up with his blond hair and wild eyes, blue eyes like I like them, eyes the color of cobalt burning on a grill . . . but Ian barges in and unplugs my Wii before I have a chance to hit save. I scream at my four-year-old cousin because he ruined everything. What a little shit. I yell, kick, throw the remote control, and scream into a pillow.

My aunt comes in because she hears Ian crying and starts yelling at me, tells me to fuck off once and for all, you disrespectful self-centered little shit, and when she leaves the next day I don't get out of bed to say goodbye.

So I'm back to my routine: Lifetime, food, Cartoon Network, porn, food, bed. One day after the next, one summer after the next, the only precious months of rest I get, the life of a kid who cries too much because his parents don't understand him, who starting in the fourth grade got left alone in his room that didn't have a door but did have a TV to watch during the day. Now summer is ending and I feel like it never happened, like the days flicked from one to the next like changing channels, one after another, praying the commercial break is quick. Tomorrow eleventh grade starts and I refuse to sleep, I fucking refuse. I want to keep watching TV until the sun comes up because I refuse to believe summer is over . . . I haven't done anything except watch TV, and somehow it's time to go back to school, back to straight A's so I can earn the right to lie around for another three months. I won't get to see what happens to Andrew on *Desperate House-wives*, the fag whose mom abandoned him in a gas station while she wept and watched him get smaller and smaller in her rearview mirror—even though I've already watched all the seasons like three times, even though I already know the lines by heart, even though I practice the scenes in front of the bathroom mirror; I still yearn for that bowl of cereal, of Frosted Flakes with chocolate milk in my bed at three in the afternoon with the fan on high, I still tear up at the thought of it, at the depth of emotion it stirs in me.

Luisito

For years Luisito thought that he would've been better off had he been born straight. He wonders whether homosexuality is his cross to bear, his destiny, to suffer a neurochemical disorder every moment of his existence: every time he wakes up with an erection after dreaming about Miguel; every morning when he runs into Emmanuel on the trolley; whenever he sees Leo with his dreads, tanned thighs, his smile that causes Luisito's legs to spread every time he sees it. For years he's yearned to feel his heart skip a beat for a pretty girl—average height, C-cup tits, high heels, makeup, long brown-banged hair—but the butterflies simply never come.

His uncles joke that he's been a fag since the womb, but no one ever mentions that to Luisito. His parents never bought him dolls whose hair he could style or dresses that would flare out as he spun. He was sent to the other room when the TV host La Comay showed a picture of a man in a green bikini and Luisito wanted to see. They never let him stay over at his friends' houses, even just to play Super Mario Bros. They kept him home, far from other boys, raising him on spankings and beatings with a belt (*Take it like a man!*), protecting the family from the shame of their strange child.

In kindergarten he put his hand down another boy's pants for the first time—Alexander, with chestnut-brown hair and a pencil dick—and they both liked the tickling and rubbing. In first grade, Jessica with the ditzy voice called him a faggot on the basketball court in front of everyone. She said faggot in English because they went to private school. If he were straight, people wouldn't insult him for no reason. In third grade they wouldn't have bullied him for twirling down the hallway with his arms in the air, wouldn't have complained to Mrs. Magda as if there were something she could do about it. In sixth grade he would have had a picture of his girlfriend taped in his locker—framed by an arrow-pierced heart drawn in black Sharpie. His formative years would have been brighter, more colorful, and free from sleepless nights.

When Luisito was twelve, his parents installed internet in the house, and he discovered porn. Around this time his pubic hair started growing like dense shrubs and he began to feel the weight of the cross on his back. In seventh grade, when he had to share a locker room with other boys, things became even more complicated. For example, Arturo: the one from the volleyball team with golden-brown hair, the one who could do one hundred push-ups in under a minute, the one whose dick was long and pointy, the one who, according to the rumors, refused to change his clothes in front of Luisito because Luisito would stare at him, rape him, taint him with his illness—his epidemic. Meanwhile Luisito tried to make himself very small, changing his clothes in a corner, facing the wall.

If Luisito had been born normal, he would have had no need to come out of the closet after meeting his first boyfriend on the internet: Hakeem, from Paterson, New Jersey. He wouldn't have written the big news (the best news of his life!) on a little scrap of paper and passed it to Graciela in history class, for Mrs. Curet to confiscate, read, and tuck into her pocket, before clenching her jaw and asking him to stay after class to discuss what she'd read. He wouldn't have felt ashamed when he saw his mother sobbing in the social worker's office; the cold and her cries wouldn't have sent a chill up his spine.

He wouldn't have wanted to disappear, wouldn't have cried whole weekends through. When Pedro the Fair rejected him, he wouldn't have carved permanent scars into his legs with the knife his grandmother used to slice tomatoes.

He always wanted to be one of the cool guys in high school, someone the other guys extended their hands to for him to shake and whom the girls greeted with a kiss on the cheek. Every day he longed to sit down at lunch and casually laugh with the other kids, with food flying from one table to the next. He longed to make offhand comments about women with tits and pussies, about how he fucked one of the girls who got around, instead of always being left out of the conversation, observing silently, measuring each syllable on his tongue so nothing he said would come out wrong and make him seem strange.

He wanted to ask a girl out, to feel a rush when she smiled and said yes, to meet her in the mall parking lot so they could go into the movie theater with the ten dollars his grandfather snuck into his pocket with a wink, to feel her cherry tongue run along his neck when the previews ended and the world went dark, and fool around until the lights came back up. Instead, because he was who he was, he settled for hiding in the back row of a shitty movie with some guy named Luigi, where they had to hurriedly pull themselves apart each time the assholes in the next row turned around to laugh.

He never doubted his sexuality, though many girls tried to convince him otherwise. Once in a while college life lent itself to drunken nights with his femme friends. He took advantage of the fact that they let him hang on them and feel their tits, sometimes right in the middle of University Avenue. Once he pinched one of their nipples and she said over and over again how drunk and horny she was; she moaned and Luisito liked it. He pressed against her jeans, squeezed her tight, pulled her against him, smelled her. Her hair, her skin, and the night inked as black as the look in her eyes ... but nothing happened. They went their separate ways and he never touched her again. His dick was half-hard, but he lost the drive: the butterflies never broke free from their cocoons.

Luisito was terrified of what his future might be like. He'd never had a "real" boyfriend or felt the warm embrace of a man's arms. He wanted to be normal so that he would never have to feel the rejection of someone like Brayan, who, after fucking Luisito and making him moan like a little slut, immediately fell asleep, leaving Luisito by his side while he snored. Luisito lay there, armor down. Never, he thought, would he ever have a normal life with five kids and go out for beers with his normal childhood friends to talk about girls; nor would he have a nice wife to give his whole heart to for fifty-plus years. He would never be free from his cross, from those muffled laughs from first grade, from that jerk Brayan who didn't want him after breaking his ass in two, from the tears that his mother had no choice but to cry for her son, her only son, who had come out like this.

FOR YEARS LUISITO thought that he would've been better off had he been born a woman. As he grew up, he noticed that he had inherited his mother's metabolism: he gained weight like a woman, in his chest and ass, as opposed to the rounded gut men in his family tended to grow. He rubbed his mother's creams on his little breasts and his butt cheeks, praying the cosmetic product would give him the tits he longed for. He began to eat more and more, despite the advice from the endocrinologist and his uncles' insults. His ass grew. By seventh grade the pants he wore to school had a size thirty-eight waist. His mother sent him to school in jeans that were skintight—on one occasion he broke a zipper, on another occasion a button popped off. One day, despite Luisito's fair skin, Juan told him that he looked like una negra preña and that he reminded him of the muffins his grandmother would make when they overflowed from their molds.

In eighth grade he focused all the hate that had been directed at him onto the space between his overgrown eyebrows. He tried to fix the problem with a pack of razors (three for three dollars), but his hand slipped and the razor got away from him more than once. This inspired another guy in class, Victor, to sing a song about his eyebrows at school in front of everyone, and Luisito's grandfather, infuriated, to berate him during the whole ride home.

And then he fixated on his hairy legs, those two inflated sausages that he wanted, more than anything, to see smooth-shaven and glistening in a pair of skanky red heels like the ones all the hot girls in class wore. He was ready: he had always walked ass sticking out, with his weight on the balls of his feet. He'd even taught his girlfriends how to strut down a catwalk. If he were a girl, he could wear tight pants without thinking twice, and everything would be perfect. A new kind of majesty: Tembandumba walking down a scintillating Antillean street, each of her earthshaking strides invoking the beating of a drum.

One day, during a family barbecue, Luisito discovered *America's Next Top Model* and nearly died at the sight of Tyra Banks, Mr. Jay, and Miss J. He emulated all the models—the most beautiful and long-legged creatures in the universe—and made a runway of the halls in his house when no one was home, a boom-boom with every step. He wanted to change the world with his pose-pose-pose in the bathroom mirror, bedroom mirror, rearview mirror. He struck poses when he got out of bed and while in the kitchen, while he "practiced" in the shower every morning; at every corner he turned, he struck a pose just in case the right audience, whose breath would be taken away, happened to be on the other side, but they never appeared. He wanted to be gorgeous like the women on the screen, though deep down he knew he never would be.

Luisito became a slave to his own image. The photographs he took of himself never came out as perfect as he imagined. His hideousness brought him to tears. He resolved to lose weight, to become slender and perfect—but neither his body, nor his metabolism, nor his perpetual hunger would cooperate. That hundred-thousand-dollar contract with Cover-Girl cosmetics slipped through his fingers. He locked himself in his room to exercise. He turned the music all the way up and danced naked with golden bangles on his wrists. He imagined he was a ballerina on the moon, free from gravity, jumping from cloud to cloud all the way to the sun, climbing his way up to the dazzling heights of Ms. Banks.

He memorized the curve that ran from her waist to her hips, her Venus body. He pulled his underwear between his butt cheeks into a Brazilian-cut thong, tucking away his genitals.

He stood on his tippy-toes because he didn't

own heels. Suddenly his legs were perfect. He turned to the side because his waist looked smaller from that angle. At the close of his nightly routine, he got in the shower and sang sad pop songs, accompanied by the sound of water hitting the ground, while sliding the bar of soap over his body to erase the memory, washing away any trace.

In the thick of adolescence, he became fed up with wondering why men didn't want him. He began to ask himself why they always chose those slutty girls who cheated on them and broke their hearts. Luisito's heart was so full of love, but there was nowhere for the love to go. If given the chance to love someone, he would cook for them, kiss them, hug them tenderly; he would satisfy their every need, always with a full belly and with their hand held . . . but unfortunately he wasn't a girl, so in school no boys ever addressed their valentines to him.

Luisito wanted to shed the fear of dressing like a woman. He was tired of standing up to urinate, of hiding his erections, of having that cumbersome thing hanging between his legs. It was something in his grandfather's face that held him back: the same reproachful look, the shame spiral. One day he would reveal himself dressed entirely in scarlet—scarlet heels, scarlet lipstick, scarlet wig. He yearned to be dainty. A princess just the right size for strong arms to wrap around and carry away from her troubles, after waking her from one hundred years of sleep with a single kiss. He didn't want to be afraid of having a boyfriend's hand rest on his waist, didn't want to worry about the red silk of his dress swelling and lifting up. Luisito would sneak away with his boyfriend when no one was looking to the back seat of a car, devour his dick, let himself be penetrated completely, his only fear that of getting pregnant rather than of getting ill with an incurable disease. He wanted to feel in control of the man, and of the universe, free from the weight of thick jackets and heavy shoes. He instead wanted to slip on a light blouse and expose his feet to the sun in golden heels, walk down the street under the bright burning light of day, showing everyone that fat asses rule this world.

FOR YEARS, Luisito thought that if he were to contract HIV, his luck might change for the better. He would never again have to suffer those twenty agonizing minutes each time he was tested, his imminent death flashing before his eyes; he would never have to be tested again. He would be released forever from the fear of catching any and all diseases. He would finally be able to die like he'd always wanted. His inevitable demise would provide for an interesting dynamic during his final days, and he'd slip into a bittersweet delirium with only his own mortality to keep him company. At last everything would be over, at last his agony would come to an end, at last he would be set free from life and all its disappointment.

He would leave home, disregarding insults from his grandmother, who blamed him for the suffering, and even for the death, of his grandfather. His departing kiss would finally soften his mother's heart and bring tears to her eyes. He would walk down the ruinous streets of Río Piedras at two in the morning when the rest of the world was asleep. Unsure of which friend to burden with his presence, he would decide it best to sleep on the street.

He would go out. He would put on a wig and steal an outfit from the women's section at Marshalls or from one of the boutiques near the Museum of Art. He would get dressed and march down the streets of Santurce in laced-up heels, with slutty cutoffs and his twenty-four-karat ass. He would exchange services for money, respond to every depraved email, post ads and prices on Adam4Adam. He would feel no fear.

He would dive headfirst into the world of drugs that had, for so long, beckoned to him with a hand made of smoke. If he only had one or two years left to live, why prolong the inevitable? Why not fatten his veins with black tar? He would cop on the most dangerous corners and they would give him little baggies filled with some white powder—hallucinogens, stimulants, dissociatives . . . He would stay out until sunrise in stilettos. He would befriend the dealers, mingle on the corners with the other street punks. He'd roam around with a crew of friends who would tie off his arm with a shoelace so he could push the needle in and feel the most intense pleasure of his life; afterward they would cuddle together to stay warm, intertwine their tongues, and exchange fluids from one body to the next. He would party forever. He would rent a dark asbestos-filled room with old paint flaking off the walls and a mattress on the floor with one set of sheets that he would never, ever change, and he would leave the door unlocked so any man could come in and pump him full of their poison whenever they felt like it. He would lie motionless all day with flies landing on his shoulders and half-open eyes.

From time to time he might cough after smoking a blunt or after climbing a flight of stairs or running for his life. He would be seen walking on the side of the road, his bones protruding from his skin, his ass saggy and flat, his face gaunt, his gaze vacant and unrecognizable. He would fall into an intense depression. Unaware even of the immense blue sky stretching out above him, he would talk to himself as if his only confidants were voices that hid in the shadows. He'd wake up out of sorts at six in the morning with diarrhea beside the La Dieciocho bus stop, fumbling over himself and falling and vomiting with his eyes fluttering closed. He'd be just another AIDS-sick vagrant haunting the streets of San Juan.

By then he would've reached rock bottom. Counting each dark patch of fungal-infected skin, he would be brought to tears as he accepted that his days were coming to an end. He'd never make it to those dance clubs—the ones he had never even laid eyes on in the heart of the city. With dicks protruding from holes in the walls ready to be sucked, with hands pulling at his arms to inject him with syringes, with drinks free of charge laced with pills and powders that would make him dance, sleep, or laugh the whole night long. He would be given crystal for his neurons so his ass would open up wide with pleasure, and the filthy room in the filthy hourly motel would disappear and he would drift back to his home, sleeping beside his grandfather like he'd done since he was little, the reason why he could never fall asleep alone.

At last he could crumble as his city had. At last he would live each day as if it were his last, to hell with tomorrow. He would stop waiting for some ride-or-die friend to rescue him from a wretched bathroom floor after having gorged himself on dick and masculine stench, because by then he would have understood that such a friend would never come, that she had forgotten all about him. He would be reduced to pure bile. He would hold up his last glass, say farewell to it all, and float out to the horizon like a cloud being carried off by a storm. He would be selfish. He would be happy. He would be flawless and fearless, transcendent.

As a result, he would wind up in the hospital after his third overdose. He would be too far gone. His white blood cells would have dropped to less than three CD4 T cells per milliliter of blood in his veins. The scabies would be eating him alive, and the nurses who cared for him would look at him with disgust, even hate. He would cough up AIDS-ridden blood and pieces of lung, he would rip out his IV and convulse on the floor, choking like a fish out of water, flailing against the weight of his own body—now as light as a feather. He would come to fulfill, at long last, his duty as a citizen of San Juan.

In Your Head

I know I should be studying, I should be holed up in my room with my backpack and books, I shouldn't be fucking up my feet with the broken glass on Robles Street . . . But it's eleven forty-seven, Bronzilocks has finally called me back, and my boredom has lost its metallic taste. We meet on the darkest corner in Río Piedras and I already feel at home. The other alcoholics and druggies on campus don't bother me anymore.

And I'm at El Bori again, waiting for the night to end. Salsa bounces off murals, thighs, outstretched necks. Earrings, bracelets, belts from another era, from thirty years ago, heirlooms taken before their time because one crisis after another kept us from filling the empty spaces in our closets. Fifteen minutes in line and I've already blown most of my rent on beer and unrequited smiles. The bartender is as dumb as they get, but he's tanned like I like them. Circus performers show up to do tricks for tips and everyone lights their blunts on the jugglers' torches. I watch from my corner, melting into the blue smoke from the Marlboro Reds, making mental notes.

Bronzilocks is back from the dead. It's been two full moons since we saw each other, the night we wanted to bathe in a river at midnight ... but that Thursday, like the start of this one, we were stuck in Santurce, the streams of the Piedras River our only tributary.

Back at my apartment, Bronzilocks opens wide for the Cosmic Space Labyrinth, a thirty-six-inch bong. She licks her glossed lips like she's confronting her first uncut, dark-skinned dick. She holds the flame to the bowl and almost loses her balance, shocked by its girth, and takes the milky stream of smoke in the back of her throat. It drips from her mouth in thick clouds. I'm so turned on I take a video of her to show people, because she doesn't want me to put it on Tumblr.

Honeyface stops being boring and joins us in the living room to complain about their exams. It's so exciting to see them finally out of their cave and smiling, for once it feels like we're actually roommates. They sit on the couch with us and my eyes are so swollen they begin to lose focus. The Labyrinth fills us up with smoke. Our house is all set up: The armchair I found one Sunday on the sidewalk. The Wii hooked up to the internet. The *Grease* soundtrack. My size-fifteen heels. Books everywhere. An overflowing ashtray. The door closed. Itching to purge the sobriety from our veins. We climb into Bronzilocks's gray Mazda 3 with Angélica, the pipe I always have on me. We fill the car with smoke and Magic 97.3, and the engine roars the whole way.

We arrive at Club 77, a dimly lit hipster bar, and others start rising from the dead. A barely recognizable face smiles at me with a lesbi-curious haircut. Panchita spots me from across the room and, like always, laughs so loud the whole dance floor hears it. Monarch kisses me on the lips. She's feeling more sensual with her new earring, she says, as she sticks the straw from her vodka grapefruit between my lips.

Honeyface says, "I'm lusting."

"After whom, pray tell?" I ask.

"That guitar player. Fuck!"

The band is so bad they have to buy their own drinks, but a drunk guy buys a Peroni for the anorexic-looking blond singer, who thinks he's in a Guess ad from the nineties. He starts grinding on whoever is closest to the stage, and I'm remembering ten, fifteen, twenty years ago when the island was in crisis as usual but there was always cable TV and milk in the fridge. Monarch summons me back to the present and we complain about losing the University of Puerto Rico's writing contest. I tell her prizes are like getting laid: you win some, you lose some, sometimes they come when you least expect it, other times they slip through your fingers.

The guitar makes our hair stand on end. Bronzilocks is busy in the corner with her ex. Honeyface is whoring around for a cigarette. The singer finally reaches peak inebriation and the band improves substantially. There's something about the pseudo-German singer: maybe it's his standard accent or his intravenous drug look; I see every vein, every river in his body. Panchita laughs in pure ecstasy. The silhouettes of other faces in the haze: dead, disappeared. Bronzilocks appears at my side, licking her wounds, and I buy us another round. We lose Honeyface to the darkness.

I find myself staring at my reflection in a

black-tinted window. There are no mirrors in my apartment. The one I had shattered during the earthquake me and a Black bottom from Atlanta caused; it couldn't take the pressure and threw itself to the floor. Now I have to look at myself in car mirrors, windows, stagnant puddles. Tonight I see my face in the dark window of Club 77, distorted by smudged fingerprints and droplets of spilled beer. I've started letting myself go, and I don't know at what point in my second, queer adolescence I let the neglect creep in.

Bronzilocks leans in with another secret: "That's how we are in the Humanities, always lost, all of us at the same time. But at least we have each other."

"Yes, girl, we are all in this crisis together."

"But, should we get used to living in shit, or overcome it?"

I don't answer. I ask myself that question every day, whether the grind is a lifestyle that is imposed or self-inflicted. I have to confess I'm getting used to the collegiate economy, to tropical poverty, to the most collective and insidious kind of scarcity. We almost made it to the top of the mountain, ten, fifteen, twenty years back, in our last childhood, in the years of

Japanese Americanization, of electronic smiles, of gray skyscrapers we could smell like smoke signals in the distance . . . but then something happened. We got left behind.

It's time to go, because this Thursday tastes the same as any other: of goodbyes, beer, and ash. I stopped going to the readings, the concerts, the markets, the cultural events, everything. I don't have a good reason. Every night I go to bed wanting something more, something I can't name, something that was always mine, but that I was always denied. I keep waiting for the flash, the asteroid, the arc spreading between clouds, the fire, the quake, the giant wave barreling toward our shore at the speed of light.

Casablanca Kush

Those assholes from Quebradillas have serious problems showing up where they say they're going to be. You all agreed to meet where every student at the University goes to smoke weed, the theater steps. You get there when you're supposed to . . . well, it's a little after nine and they said eight thirty, but this is Puerto Rico: time flows differently in the Caribbean, where summer never ends and the months melt together into one long hot day. Everyone on the theater steps forks over two bucks for blunts, and someone says that's probably why those broke-asses are nowhere to be found. Convenient for Booty (whose real name is Bobby, but it's more satisfying to think of the quality of his ass, with the meatiest cheeks in the Natural Sciences department), who is a kleptomaniac with seemingly more extremities than an octopus. His first tentacles grew at age four when he stole a pack of the same

condoms his dad used; he even had the fore-
sight to stick them in his sister's baby bottle so
she could sip strawberry-flavored milk.

You call them, and Booty answers—they've
already left. All they do is get high, so why
is it so hard for them to stay put and smoke
their half ounce like good little stoners? Now
they're at Pueblo in Hato Rey and Booty is
about to do what Curbelo and Mr. Postmodern said he pulled off last weekend: steal over
a hundred dollars of Chilean wine, which
apparently is as easy as one person keeping
watch while the other slips bottle after bottle
into Curbelo's bag—a messenger bag covered
in pro-legalization pins that he's been using
since freshman year. The alcohol aisle, to the
disservice of the store and the benefit of the
worshippers of Bacchus, is situated directly out
of the security camera's sight line. As for you,
the only things you're brave enough to steal
are books, pens, wallets from Hot Topic, and
women's earrings from Macy's. Those fuckers.

You agree to meet them at Curbelo's apartment—not because of the wine but because
La Puta Astuta swears to have acquired the
most exquisite, hair-raising herb to have ever
graced Boricua soil. So much sweet saliva

fills her glands that she can't resist telling us the legend she received in a yellowed envelope, delivered that very day by a UPS worker, along with a box wrapped in golden velvet. La Puta Astuta has gorgeous legs; they were the first thing you noticed one random day when you saw that bitch step on the bus, smooth-shaven, Desi complexion, and the sunglasses of an heiress checking into rehab. In the pose of a mermaid contemplating the horizon from the cliffs of Quebradillas, she starts telling us the story of weed so potent, so sensationally dank, that at the first whiff a group of explorers on the Orinoco River split into two groups to seek its source. It was so similar to the scent of their wives' snatches back home that they trailed the perfume like hounds, scouring the virgin landscape, penetrating swamps plagued with crocodiles and forests infested with panthers until, five days later, some seven survivors lost consciousness when hit with the stench emanating from a small handful of cannabis plants hidden from the world in a tiny meadow, an eye in the hurricane of the pre-Columbian Amazon. Their leaves were so red and their buds so golden that they resembled giant hibiscus flowers imported from Jupiter.

Only one survivor, by some miracle, made it back to camp after being spit out of the forest's darkness, clutching a single plant he'd dug up by the roots. Wild-eyed, his iron armor dented and his body covered in scratches, claw marks, and infected insect bites (his face was so swollen that one of his eyes completely disappeared, according to the written accounts), he begged for refuge from the beasts and pests lured by the intoxicating perfume. That night he slept with the buds clutched to his chest as they whispered thanks to him for freeing them from the labyrinthine depths of the forest. The buds turned out to be cursed: upon the explorers' return to the Canary Islands, a hurricane wreaked havoc on the Atlantic waters, a storm so powerful it has yet to be matched. The explorer locked himself in his cabin to protect his small satchel of golden buds and little red seeds, ignoring the crew's screams and the storm and the subaquatic thumping of the Kraken—

"Girl, you're tripping!" you say, holding out your hand so she'll pass you the blunt.

"My bad," she answers, flashing perfect teeth. "Apparently I have some family in Morocco, or so I found out this week when this package came addressed to me. I'm not shitting you, my first thought was 'Hmm, from Morocco? It'd better be weed.' And what do you know, I open it up and there's like this little scroll with the legend that you didn't let me finish and some instructions telling me that the four ounces inside the coffee cans should be rolled and smoked tonight, during the spring equinox, in the name of the soldiers of Titicaca, I think that's what they were called, before the imperial forces of King Iztukmambarorwhateverthefuck come to take back what's theirs."

"Dude, four ounces?" Mr. Postmodern says, with eyes like a prowling animal.

"From Morocco?" you say.

"All of it? In one night?" Curbelo says, even though he supposedly quit smoking.

"I guess, because if we don't, 'the consequences will be catastrophic' or something like that. Whatever, it's four ounces that I got for free. Why not spread the love?"

"Okay, I'll smoke the blunts," Booty says, making himself comfortable on the floor, brushing the leftover ashes from the theater steps from the seat of his pants.

"We can roll them at my place," Curbelo says. "Come by after class around eight thirty."

"That gives me enough time to stop home and eat," you say, thinking of the twink from Sacred Heart University who told you he wants you to fuck him tonight after six, but you know it probably won't happen.

"Perfect, let's do it," La Puta Astuta says. "Today's Thursday, right?"

"Ayo, we gotta hand them out tonight at El Bori, for sure," you add, passing the blunt.

And just like that a plan was hatched. But those queens never answer their phones, and you smoke in the meantime, and forget about the rice on the stove until it's so burnt you throw it in the trash along with the destroyed pot. The twink from Sacred Heart flakes because he has a chemistry exam, and now these evil sons of bitches aren't at Curbelo's apartment and you call Mr. Postmodern just to listen to it ring until finally the voice of his roommate Reggieman answers to inform you that they are all in his apartment on Humacao Street, waiting for La Puta Astuta to get there with the weed. You tell them they are evil sons of bitches who don't let anyone know when they change their plans, and he says, after laughing at how mad you are, that you'd better hurry up before all the weed is gone. All right, you fly low over Muñoz

Rivera Avenue and when you get there, they greet you with the brusque effusiveness of a straight man greeting a fag he's fond of: they scream *Hey Biiiitch!* and hug you and grab your ass. You don't return the gesture.

On the counter there are several metal cylinders so polished that the reflection from the light hurts your eyes. "Coffee cans?" you ask, but La Puta Astuta shows you a copy of the inheritance papers, a tome that bestowed to her, by royal decree of her great-uncle Abdullah or whatever the fuck his name was, the four ounces, along with the story of the Flower of Abdullah III and a rough translation from Arabic from another century written on what can only be described as a scroll. You try to decipher what appears to be a curse from the last Amazonian king of the Triticocu but Booty and Curbelo show up with two boxes of cheap cigars and five bottles of wine clanking in Curbelo's bag.

"You both are honest-to-god angels," you say, grateful that you've managed to become part of their group.

La Puta Astuta starts going on about how you all need to be careful because those documents are real and very serious, and she doesn't want any problems with anyone. Mr. Postmodern and Reggieman start opening the cigars and emptying their insides into a small maggot-filled trash can. Booty opens a bottle and Curbelo passes out teacups filled with wine. You sit down to read the scroll and everything La Puta Astuta said is laid out on the parchment, written in flowery Arabic text in ink the color of coagulated blood and covered in a reddish dust. According to the legend, there were no survivors from the shipwreck, just one barrel that washed up on the Moroccan shore a few months later with a bag of buds and a final testament from the Canarian explorer (dated October 7, 1780) in which he narrates the nights of torment in the jungle and begs that the seeds never, ever be planted in fertile soil.

"All right, we ready?" La Puta Astuta says, snatching the papers from your hand.

"I've always dreamed of smoking kush from Morocco," Reggieman answers.

"Lezdoit."

This bitch starts reading in some fake-ass Arabic. Curbelo interrupts with the suggestion that La Puta place one hand on the coffee can and read like she's praying, like she's mad as hell, like she's in the cockpit of a crashing plane.

She does. It sounds like a magic incantation and it raises the hairs on your skin. The lights in the apartment flicker and a salty wind blows through the crack in the door, which makes no sense because we are in Santa Rita, where the only smells the wind carries are piss and cat shit from the sidewalk. When La Puta finishes, a gust slams the front door shut and the coffee-can lid slowly begins to unscrew itself, which is fucking unsettling, unleashing a thick rose-colored smoke that hovers above the can. The sickly-sweet smell makes you hard, and you sit on the ground to try to hide it. You notice that everyone else seems weak in the knees. It smells super-extra fruity, a mix of strawberry-orange-lemon-mango, so potent it fills the whole shitty apartment. La Puta Astuta ties a black bandana around her face, puts on a pair of cobalt-blue sunglasses, and sends us to our respective battle stations.

The golden nuggets are intoxicating: shining, spongy, and sparkling from little THC crystals so they look like sugarcoated fruit. La Puta inspects each bud, every centimeter of their surfaces, using a magnifying glass to study the leaves' pink-veined matrices that are revealed under direct light. You and

Curbelo hold your breaths while the others, with sorrow in their hearts, break up the buds with their fingers. They feel like leaves picked off wild plants on Playa Escondida—delicious! Reggieman and Mr. Postmodern mix the weed with tobacco, their eyes shining from their hypnotic highs.

"Bobby, don't even think about taking a picture of those buds," La Puta snaps. "Roll the blunts, you fat bastard!" And in two hours we have a few hundred blunts ready to be handed out to the masses.

On the way to El Bori, Booty asks why we don't just sell the blunts. He makes a good point, but you've never cared for that particular underground market. It goes against some personal philosophy you adopted in high school when you first started smoking, that weed is a plant that grows free and should stay that way, if for no other reason than to slow the wave of crime that's left this island a no-man's-land. You agree when La Puta replies that no one here is going to pay the thousand-plus dollars each blunt is worth: that's to say, they're priceless. You look at Mr. Postmodern and you both have tears in your eyes; aware that you are moments from the best blaze of your lives, you link arms and start jumping like two teenage girls getting high for the first time. It's midnight and El Bori is packed enough for your crew to begin your mission. You even overhear people whispering, between shots of Jack and coconut, that someone is wandering downtown Río Piedras with the dankest weed ever to have crossed Caribbean waters, that they've opened their stash and rolled a few blunts, tormenting the poor souls scraping by on a student budget. You were taught to always share your wealth with your fellow citizens, and seeing so many starving students, you're pleased La Puta agrees and is handing out her inheritance to those starving dopefiends.

A small circle begins to form around you and La Puta as she opens the loot. (What a joy to think that the lions of Zion blessed her with all these blunts!) One by one the drunken patrons turn their faces in your direction and join the crowd. They look like a group of horny penguins in collective masturbation, with La Puta on her knees in the center, and inch forward with tentative steps, like vultures closing in on a cheetah whose insides have been ripped out. You resist turning around, grabbing the weed before it's too late, taking it to the beach, and celebrating every twentieth of April in history. Just then, the jukebox cuts out and more people start coming down from the balcony in your direction. The murmurs, the questions, the desperate look in their eyes. The vultures look ready to swoop in at any moment. You whisper to La Puta that maybe this mission wasn't such a good idea after all.

"Blunts! Blunts for whoever wants one! Come and get 'em!" La Puta starts to shout, tossing a handful into the air.

Mayhem breaks loose. People squeal like bridesmaids as they snatch the bouquets midair. They gather on the pavement around you ready to shed blood for blunts. Some drop their beers on the pavement and they explode, adding to the chaos. The most desperate among them risk their hands being stomped on to reach down and pick up even the bloodiest blunts. Something about the night, about the full moon hanging low in the cloudless sky, the mural of giant graffitied eyes behind El Bori, adds an even more ominous atmosphere to the scene. You get shoved around until you lose sight of your friends. You hear the first blunts being lit and when you look up you're next to a guy who has a look in his eye so fierce that you hide the two blunts in your hand for fear he might rip your arm clean off.

"Damn, that was you who rolled up with all those blunts? Got any left?"

He moves in too close; you smell Jack Daniel's on his breath; something in his eyes, in his sexy gut, stirs your hormones. You get an idea.

"If you let me suck your dick, I'll give them to you."

A look of rage flashes across his face but is quickly extinguished. He looks at his watch and contemplates the offer, like it's a marble he's rolling around on his tongue.

"Okay, let's go over there," he says so quietly you barely hear. You grab his arm before he has time for a second thought.

You float off with the clouds of smoke, and sighs of relief, of pleasure, are exhaled all around you. You lead him to a vacant lot next to El Bori where they sometimes project movies, and you push him against a wall, far from any electric light. You hand him the first blunt. When you get on your knees to unbutton his jeans, you begin salivating, because he's already half-hard, not too thick, but a good seven inches in length that fit perfectly into your mouth.

Salty, just how you like it. He lets out a moan; whether it's caused by the smoke hitting his lungs or your oral faculties, you can't be sure. Viva universal weed! Far off you hear screams. Screams of terror? Like the sounds of strange animals, followed by shattering glass. You play with the hair below his belly button, move up to pinch his nipples, tangle your fingers in the wild foliage under his arms. His dick gets fat with blood as you work. He pushes you to the ground, into a dirty piss-filled puddle. You look up to find his chest covered in thick black fur, his muscles growing so much his clothing is torn to shreds, and his nose pushing out into a snout with a row of sharp-pointed teeth below it. Suddenly you find yourself defenseless and about to be devoured by a goliath he-wolf howling his canine lament under the silver light of the full moon.

Out of nowhere a guaraguao twice his size swoops down, grabbing him with its talons, ripping out his intestines midflight, and bathing you in his thick blood before flying off toward El Bori. You can't make sense of what's happening but the scent of weed is stronger than ever and a saccharine smoke is crawling through the streets, the same smoke that crawled out of that coffee can. You run back toward the chaos and the first thing you see is a pink rhino with an ass so wide its cheeks brush against the buildings on either side of the street and a face so sad (though, in all honesty, how sad can a pink rhino look?) that you swear you see tears in its eyes as it runs by. A pack of derelicts passing blunts back and forth disintegrates before your eyes into a pile of cockroaches that scurry into the gutter. A few preppy girls stand frozen, then rip off their arms to shoot bullets out of their shoulders like machine guns. Reggieman appears and is spinning like a blender with a continuous stream of smoke coming from his mouth; he drills into the asphalt so fast it cracks the pavement, creating a great fissure. A bunch of mutants and circus beasts crawl out of it, monsters straight out of the movies: thirty-foot copperhead anacondas battling giant squids that hang from the lampposts, marble elephants with three trunks thrashing in the air to fight off millions of metallic wasps, eight-legged sheep climbing the walls, spitting fire at Mr. Postmodern's legs as he screams his girlfriend's name into the crowd. You feel a nibbling at your calf and see a sand-colored chihuahua with a black bandana around its neck; you snatch it up to protect it from an oncoming antelope stampede but it continues to bark and bite, so you hold it out in front of you and it lets out a stream of piss, and when you throw it in the air toward the screams and smoke, it explodes into a puff of fuchsia glitter.

Next you see Curbelo transform into a wax statue, one hand on his hip and the other holding a Benson. Damn, hadn't Curbelo quit smoking? What made him fall off the wagon? You'd admired him, your only friend who tried to kick bad habits. You light his wick to melt him and end his misery. That's when you snap out of it and start shouting in desperation because you don't see any of your other friends and don't understand what the fuck is going on. You run around El Bori screaming *fiiiiire-fiiiiirrree!* but there's no one there, just amorphous beings groaning from the pain of transforming—not into animals anymore but into creatures from another world. You climb up a pile of bodies and step onto the roof, above the murals, searching in the fog for another soul. Nothing. You throw yourself facedown and pray for the nightmare to end, that death is kinder on you than it's been on the others.

And then a thought occurs to you: What better way to relieve pain than to smoke some weed? Fuck it. You pull a blunt out of your pocket and light it with a trembling hand just as a boom resounds over Río Piedras and the city's power grid goes black. In the darkness, you can only hear tires screeching from University Avenue, and the howling of a beast from what sounds like the Earth's very core. You feel the smoke penetrate your lungs. It smells so sweet, with its pineapple-mango tang, that you burst into tears from the unparalleled ecstasy; by the third drag a fire scrapes its fingernails along your veins and burns your bones from the inside. Your skin turns gray, scaly; a tail bursts through the seam of your pants; your tongue unfurls down to your stomach; you begin to identify the smells of leather and salted cod and molten metal and teenage musk floating in the air. Claws sprout from the hand holding the blunt and you use them to climb up the side of a building to a window where you see your reflection, a giant reptile with a pitch-black tongue.

You use your new feet to cross the small bridge over Gándara Avenue and in the blink of an eye you're scaling the University's bell tower. From the new height, San Juan looks like an ocean of fire and mushroom-shaped clouds. Your tongue picks up the scent of the flames billowing from the gas stations. The guaraguaos pierce the silence with their hungry battle cries. Your head whips toward the sound of two men stumbling out of an alley a block away from the Humanities buildings, their pants still around their ankles, frightened and yelling about the incessant explosions and the quaking earth. Humanities students understand hunger better than anyone. With an innate stealth, you slither between tangled vines and, once you're close enough to them, you grab one of the men with your tongue, dragging him into the shadows. The other one shrieks and takes off running while you devour his lover, licking what's left of his bowels from your claws.

Once you finish you climb back up the tower to keep watch over the bell. You stay there without knowing why. Something compels you. You're getting used to your new reptilian body. Your bones feel lighter. Your eyes are still bloodshot from the weed, but now you can pull them back and hide them in your skull. Soon you'll shed your skin. You're cold, but it's almost dawn, and you'll recover your strength. This new form is going to last a while, and you don't mind. With your new eyes, colors fragment into unending waves, in strange and delirious new hues. You can even make out the explosions near the coast. Now it's your turn to protect the half blunt that remains because it's all you've got, and they don't sell dime bags to dragons.

Devilwork

Perhaps I should write about Alain . . . He always shows up late for French—later than me, at least. Monsieur Sebbana, the Algerian professor with the hairy, veiny biceps, immersed as he is in his relative pronouns, makes no note of the slight breeze that is Alain as he shows up reeking of indica, all pallor and emaciation wrapped in black tunics, copper-bleached hair, and an iciness about him, epitomized by his glacier-ringed irises. A poet, so he often says, and I concur, despite his being nineteen. Alain sits down at an angle without taking out a notebook, lays his eyes on me like an invisible weight, and starts stroking his bulge with a subtlety that only I and Monsieur Sebbana notice. Monsieur Sebbana turns back to the board and pulls up his jeans to cover his butt beard. I look away, thinking I barely have any time to turn in this story I'm supposed to be working on for Doctor Townshend, who gets tired of giving extensions despite respecting our own unique creative processes and what-not, so he says, and Monsieur Sebbana won't stop looking over his shoulder in my direction. *Je sais qui tu es*, I communicate telepathically with a wink, and he drops his chalk, bends over, and picks it up again. Alain taps his pen sharply three times on his desk so that I'll look at him, but I won't give him the satisfaction. I haven't even started writing the story—it has to be a matryoshka, whatever that means . . . Is that the right word?

Alain has given me a few stories in the past—and I've thought about him long enough to make up a few of my own—but I can't recall one that really does him justice. Just another Hispanic Studies major, still pursuing an academic career with aplomb, melancholy as a result of the war on drugs we were born into, both of us fatherless and destined to never stray too far from our respective grandmothers' homes. We half-bonded throughout our first-year writing seminar, digesting mammoth novels and revolutionary poetry while surviving off black coffee and American Spirits. These days we usually meet after French to make fun of some student's faux pas, which the professor likes to correct with dismissive hand waves or puffs of hot air. In my head I muse about how musty or salty Alain's nuts must smell and taste when we're on our way to grab a coffee and practice whatever sick grammar trick we just learned in class.

Monsieur Sebbana asks us to describe a picture of a goat pen in the textbook, the goat farm he grew up on, he jokes. He asks us to recite the sentences we come up with in our rudimentary French, but I can't stop thinking about last Thursday when Alain and I went out. We met at my place for bong hits and Lorca. He confessed he was raised Pentecostal, and I shuddered at the thought; I can't even, but there's a story if I ever needed one: haggard Alain, guided by the Holy Ghost, expelling some unnamable demon, while the congregation stomps and dips and drums away. Once we were too high to function, we walked toward the inner-city neon lights for some lo-fi rock show he couldn't miss, but we still had to walk his friend Nicole to her car because she was tired of waiting for the band to find their coke and start the show, and Alain thinks of her as defenseless so he wouldn't let her leave by herself—so I had to wait while they finished making out, huddling under some forgotten streetlight, flickering till it cut out into darkness.

Then we finally dove into Club 77's harried red mist, and the band started playing. Alain paid for our drinks, despite the self-imposed poverty he says gives his poems their acidity—and here's where I could start the story: with both of us sitting at the bar near the mosh pit, two unmoving statues, incapable of crossing the individual cones of silence under which we fester. Here comes the story within a story: *Alain was molested by a cousin five years older*, or something like that, something to explain those demonic voices bouncing off the club's concrete walls or how so many remarkable verses could have been written in a world so garbled in dark speech—he thinks so, at least. And this other narrative intermingles with mine, my own untold stories, and how these drunk, crashing bodies on the floor release their deep-seated aggressions, remind him of his older cousin who lived three doors down, pull me toward writhing on the floor with him—how years of abuse translate into teen angst, reckless nights hunting down dawns, inner thighs hiding self-inflicted scars—how he showed me those scars once, he couldn't bear how his secrets weighed him down, he felt the symptom of some sinful disease slowly creeping down his spine night after night, ripping him out of the conscious world—and once the tears start running, once I too feel them rolling down my cheeks, I pull him out of Club 77 and pray for relief from the night's wicked blade, beg him to tell me what happened so long ago only to have him rest all his lankiness over me, pinning me down on some street corner—and I figure this is the only way I'll get him to want me, in a drunken stupor expelling his demons through whispers into my hair, and he reaches into my pants despite my drunken protests and the act triggers horrible memories from my own past, and his neck jerks back and he sees ghosts dancing in my eyes but I cover his mouth with mine and now he's the one pinned down, now he's mine for me to devour and I can see the images from his past flash before his eyes—*there* I could place the story within the story, or should it be woven into the general storyline?—*no*, what the hell, that's not a story within a story, that's just me being sick in the fucking head like most days—

"Votre phrase?" Monsieur Sebbana asks me again, his thighs pressed to the edge of my seat.

The professor's question bounces off the whiteboard, off the classroom's concrete walls, inside my skull, so many times in an instant. "Excusez-moi?"

"Votre phrase. Les paysans, ont-ils acheté combien de chèvres? As-tu la réponse?"

"Ah, oui, oui, la phrase . . . Quelle page?"

Out of the corner of my eye, I see Alain smiling at my futile attempts to buy time. But I can't respond to him or acknowledge the way he holds his long dickprint for me to see. One hungry glance and he'll know instantly what I have planned for him, how I'll write his story into mine. I can't take it. I find the page in the workbook and guess at the answer, and the professor, brows furrowed, pounces on the next student. We spend the final minutes of class reviewing for next week's test, and as soon as we're dismissed, I chase after Alain—but keeping track of the possessed is harder than it seems, and he's gone without a trace.

I COULD WRITE about my Portuguese professor, Doutora Morães. I mean, she's not that good of a professor. She's really a psychologist, not a linguist, and I have plenty of intense grammar questions that my other professors are quick to answer, but she usually seems too flustered to come up with a good explanation and I have to just google it. But she tries hard, and her hips jiggle intolerably under her tropical cotton dresses whenever she erases the whiteboard, which she seemingly does constantly as she's so eager to overexplain everything; she's always writing on the board with her wide hands always clawing at the air with red stiletto nails, or even with her broad always-exposed shoulders winking at me, as if she were scratching her own back wishing it was me, so I feel like I should try to match her efforts.

Without Alain to distract me, I show up on time to class. I figure that if I learn Portuguese, get good grades in most of my classes, work on my shit and save up some money living with my grandmother, I'll get into grad school at the Universidade de São Paulo—no, better yet, Universidade Federal do Rio de Janeiro, somewhere I can find asteroid-like rocks sticking out of the surf, with Cariocas that don't wax their taints, whose meaty hips burst out of canary-yellow thongs—like Leticia from XVideos roller-skating down the burning noon sidewalk with her chocolate curls blowing in the breeze, like Janderson's shea-buttered thighs thick as billboards, immortalized in some of Pornhub's highest rated videos. But I can't get over Doutora Morães, that unbearable way she shows up late for class after lunch with guava pastry still crumbling from her mouth, a complete one-eighty from what Tumblr says a bombshell Brazilian teacher in thick-rimmed glasses should look like.

I'm tired of getting off to some staticky image at two a.m. wishing it were Doutora Morães, huddled in silence in the corner of my room, wasting away from insomnia and hunger. I want the saltiness of flesh, tongues snaking across necks and shoulders—what better than porn to tell a story within a story? Okay, what's one more porn fantasy about a teacher, what harm? Doutora Morães's body tells me another story, bodacious and fluid but always slightly off whenever I stay after class to ask her about some odd conjugation I didn't quite get, letting me know that she's bracing for it when she sits down on the desk in such a way that it barely creaks. She adjusts her glasses and sticks her tongue out of the corner of her mouth as she bends forward to read the notes I'm showing her, and I can smell the pêssego body lotion on her sweaty sunspotted tits. She laughs at the fantasies I wrote about her in class and actually takes the notebook to circle certain words with a red pen, occasionally throwing her curls back in laughter, braying almost like a goat, but a flirty goat that likes being pursued. She keeps reading and her expression gets serious; she looks up at me, then back at the notebook.

Doutora Morães takes out her phone to show me a video of her jumping up and down during carnival in Bahia, where she's from, or maybe in La Perla in Old San Juan, so many films mix together in my memory, though she's probably with the dance group she never stops raving and reminiscing about, As cabras loucas—which I'm guessing she named herself due to her contagious-if-unnerving laughter. I can hear the batucadas in the background when a muscled, curly-haired arm wraps around her waist and pulls her closer to him and raises the back of her skirt, and she rubs her closed fist up and down her crotch. They're surrounded by a dense crowd bopping to the drums and pushing closer together. From the way her tits are bouncing I can tell the dude behind her is having the carnival of his life, and she grabs the phone to record from a better angle how that thick dick keeps going in and out of her. At this point I'm shaking and trying hard not to look at her sitting on the desk subtly raising the hem of her dress when the camera turns again and it's me in the crowd with them, also taking dick from the back, and she stares at me hard imagining what it must feel like to be railed like that during a procession on a hot Saturday afternoon in February.

I pull out my phone and show her a video of my own, one I took of her in class this one time she shared a new funk track by some music producer friend of hers. She starts dancing for us, and her ass jiggles uncontrollably under the thin fabric of her dress. She flushes red staring at the video on my phone, but she knows that I'm looking at her and only her. In the video she persists and moves about uncomfortably and looks quite nervous after a minute once everyone else in the background stops laughing, but I also think she's enjoying this very moment, us alone in her fifty-square-foot classroom with broken chairs and rarely any markers, let alone a working projector. As she keeps watching the video on my phone (she really did dance around for over three minutes, but we all learned something that day), I get down on my knees and pull up the hem of her dress, dive in face first, and lick the sticky silky bulge on her large, high-waisted red panties—I look up at her and she's recording me with my phone in her right hand while she shows me another video of her getting railed at Carnival but closer to sunset, and I grab my phone to record the look on my face as I stare at her and lick larger and larger circles around her crotch—*Isso, isso, caralho, prova oral, passou a prova oral*, she moans before braying hard—and before I know it Doutora Morães has set up a light ring and two tripods for both of our phones and lies down on the desk while I straddle her and—

"Oi! No que você está pensando?" Doutora Morães asks while she walks past my seat, peering at my notebook.

"Prova oral, quero a prova oral," I hear myself say.

Literally everyone stops what they're doing and stares at me. Someone even drops their phone.

"O que?"

"Ohmygah—whatdidIsay?" I answer, quickly disposing of the page I rip out as if that were the reason for my confusion.

"Você fez a tarefa?"

"Fiz, professora, sim."

Then I read some random sentence she points out in my textbook and I somehow guess the right answer.

"Obrigada," she says, a tad hushed.

"Pois não, professora . . . Imagina."

She looks back at me with a raised eyebrow, launching me a lightning bolt with a wink, and returns to attend to the other students.

No more pornos. Enough with fantasies about professors. I almost got in trouble for the last one. They rarely go viral anyways.

MAYBE I SHOULD just settle for writing about my cousin Charlie, who is currently studying opera in Leipzig. Before my mother died, Charlie and I would play together at my aunt's goat farm. My aunt was a world-class musician and one of the few women cuatristas in Isabela. Charlie would sing along during parrandas and as he got older would carry around a portable speaker and a microphone. I remember him being a violent child that threw rocks at the goats to hear them bleat and pushed me or other cousins into the nearby creek. Only music or his mother's cuatro seemed to soothe him. His dad was an alcoholic and never around. We would run to the sand dunes at sunset and every now and then wrestle each other to the sand, straddle each other, stick our hands in each other's shorts, pin the other down and bite the other's neck as hard as we could. I once spoke to my aunt frankly about the sunset roughhousing that Charlie and I would get into, and I suddenly had to move to San Juan with my grandmother. Charlie and I lost touch after that.

Once Tumblr shut down its X-rated content, I joined the great migration to other freak social-media platforms, and soon enough the algorithm brought me to Charlie's Twitter. I knew it was him because his old Tumblr featured naked furries fucking in tropical forests, like foxes or cows or zebras humping each other, explicitly celebrating interspecies erotica in some of the riskier videos. The coarse-haired, sinewy forearms, the dark tanned skin and even darker balls overgrown with bush, the stick-and-poke Taurus neck tattoo, the enormous curly-horned beast mask with glowing red eyes—they all screamed Charlie, and the archive that he'd lost on Tumblr he was gradually sharing on Twitter. He accumulated over 50K followers in two years.

I'm embarrassed to admit that to this day I get off while reading the fantasies he writes, handle @meFFistoFFelesPR. He uploads vids of himself and his masked furry friends in Vienna or in Frankfurt at an underground, lasered discotheque. Or vids of himself squatting on shockingly large squashes or cucumbers. His hole gapes like a hairy puckered ring as it engulfs everything in its path. Or the micronarratives he writes about his Krampus character fucking celebrities, complete with doctored pics of these same celebrities naked and being horn penetrated. Or popper training vids that he edits and records himself, interspersed with pictures of black goats or pentacles or fisting videos. I can tell he's a storyteller, that he must be very verbal in bed, that he has to find a way of constructing a narrative through every sexual impulse he strings together day by day. I bet I could take one of his stories and run with it for Doctor Townshend's assignment.

While watching Charlie's videos, I like to pour warm coconut oil all over my crotch and rub vegetables against myself until I nut over a stuffed goat I've had since I was a child. This semester I only have afternoon classes, so I get to stay up late as Charlie updates his followers on his escapades. He's trying to rack up followers for his OnlyFans and is accepting requests for video calls for a small fee, so he dares to share online. My Twitter has no posts, no retweets, no profile pictures: only 27.7K likes and counting. I knew however that this would turn him on.

"You ever fuck with those horns?" I DM him.

"I only fuck with my horns," Charlie answers after three minutes. "Any pics?"

I send him a shot of my unshaven taint, legs up. He sends back a selfie and I nearly spill my jasmine tea—it really is Charlie. I send him my favorite picture of Alain.

"Damn you're hot, are you Puerto Rican?"

"Yeah, though my mom is from Long Island, and I know you are too."

"How can you tell?"

"Your likes, your retweets, your hairy balls, your fantasies. Big bugarrón vibes."

"So you like islander bicho."

"I like islander fist."

"Hell yeah," he says, and sends me a picture of his hairy, veiny forearms. "I do grip and wrist curls every day."

"Cabrón, I really don't care about your fore-arm routine."

"Okay nevermind."

"Wait tell me more," I backtrack. As fickle as a goat, it would seem.

"About what."

"Name a person you've always wanted to fist."

"My cousin."

I spit my tea all over the university library computer screen and keyboard. Luckily no one is around on a Saturday morning, so I quickly kill the power and run out the door, into the downpour despite my short shorts and flip-flops, and head to the clock tower on campus, getting as close as I can in hopes that some bone-jarring chiming bell will shake me back into myself.

The ding-ding-dongs at noon finally do the trick. I pull out my phone.

"Why your cousin?"

"I wanna see the little bitch squirm. Wanna fill that big mouth all the way up."

"Squirm how hard?" I see my fingers type.

"Hard enough that they burst open and push my fist out."

"Wait, before that—what else would you do to your cousin? They hot?"

"Very hot. Their taint is hairy like yours." I think Charlie knows.

"How do you know?"

"I found their freak Twitter."

Charlie doesn't know shit.

"What else would you do to them?"

"I would clamp their nipples."

"Boring."

"I would fuck them with my horns."

"Wearing the horns or actually fucking with the horns?"

"Actually with the horns."

"In which hole?"

"Down your throat, up your nose."

"Don't play dumb, what else."

"Geile Sau, qué rico, I would take them to the sand dunes in Isabela, real early like seven a.m., and dig a hole in the sand so that their upper half is buried like an ostrich and I'm in my full Krampus gear fisting their gaping hole and the sound it makes ohmygod, such a wet sucking sound as I go as deep as my elbow, and when they're done nutting I kick sand on them, kannst ich pisse in deinem Arsche, then I do—"

And the voice note he was suddenly possessed enough to send to me cuts off just as he finishes breathing out my name in noisy, greedy bleating sounds that startled the phone right out of my hand. Despite so many years avoiding the images seared behind my eyelids, I return to the same scene when I was five and Charlie had buried me up to my neck in sand, when he made me drink his own piss before he unburied me and decided not to anyway. Before I block Charlie, I screen-record the entire exchange, voice note and all. I'll find a use for this story in some later family event, or at his graduation recital.

THIS STORY IS due tomorrow. I can only dwell and pace around for so long before I feel invaded by their memory, succubused by their desire projected toward me. And here I am on Dirtyroulette, settings on Puerto Rico, conducting research for my latest idea, my own story invaded by the handful of gooners awake at four a.m. also reaching for the small brown bottle between their legs or on their solar plexus and raising it to each nostril, my own story expanding exponentially through every faceless naked torso rubbing one out—but that's not a story within a story, I keep freaking out about form—like this new window into an air-conditioned library, an older salt-and-pepper daddy like I like them, the camera upturned just to show some beard and a neck tattoo, a tattoo that starts to become more familiar with every hit of poppers, and I cover the trackpad in coconut oil as I stop to expand the image and, yes, that is Doctor Townshend's octopus neck tattoo, that is his salt-and-pepper beard, this is the story I've been hoping to find this entire time. But I have to stop, I have to close the laptop and accept defeat. What are the chances. This island is entirely too small for comfort.

Perhaps I *should* write about Doctor Townshend ...

The Blunts That Bond Us

Seeing it on an MTV pseudodocumentary isn't the same as living it firsthand. It's only when we tear up our own hearts and scatter them like ashes in the wind that we can fathom all the love that's truly possible. After all those years of failed attempts—of half-hearted fucks, of muttering insults—new constellations finally form in the night sky. How many times have I seen myself almost out from under the shadow of loneliness, toward intimacy, toward those seaquakes that flood my bowels and return the pulse to my kidneys, sucking me into the glowing TV screen until early Monday morning. They take away my hunger and return it in one blow, knocking the wind out of me. What do I do with myself . . . What do I do with all the hours that lie ahead?

I admit my jealousy is immature. An emerald lizard crawling across my inner thigh, whispering secrets into my ribs. Leo lying with his head in Edwin's lap. Leo staying at Edwin's house for two days. Leo buying chicken breasts at ECONO for the two of them to cook during the week. Leo smiling and flashing secret glances at Edwin, and both thinking I don't notice, failing to take into account that my vision has evolved and I can sense their every movement even at the very edge of my periphery. I freeze on the theater steps, every detail imprinted in my mind as if I were watching a bus driving against traffic at top speed, with my stomach in knots that keep me from eating. I imagine that I'm a fly soaring toward its own death, flying straight into the electrical storm that claps in the space between their gazes. Sometimes I die inside when I see them together like that, so far from me and so close to each other in their own world, so ephemeral in the square frame of their infatuation, while my cubic loneliness crystallizes. Sometimes I dedicate an entire sleepless night to them, digging into the skin of my fingertips and ripping out the bones, sighing confessions into the darkness that I would never utter in the light of day. They have their own fantasies— just the two of them, and I hate it.

It sucks to share a group of friends with my

two lovers, especially when they don't realize that they're both my lovers.

I DON'T PLAN on leaving the house this morning. Portuguese class can wait. I forgot to order my Buspirone and now my anxiety has me shaking. And I'd been fine for weeks! We'd finally cleared the air after the drama from the Bad Decision Club's most recent carnal delirium, and I'd found some semblance of normalcy to start the semester with: arriving ten minutes early to class in the mornings, freezing my ass off in the library until midnight, handing in my exams in record time . . . until one day my world collapsed. And I was left alone with a block of ice where my chest used to be.

Seventeen hours and forty-five minutes ago Edwin was drawing a fractal pattern on Leo's bicep.

That knotted muscle, with its veins charting maps of life and tangled hairs that, one fleetingly eternal night, grazed my stretch-marked torso. Edwin has a knack for drawing and fills his notebooks with sketches of old people rolling cigarettes, with anime characters staring out wide-eyed from the page, with super-complicated fractals stretching out of a black hole. I saw the first spark in Leo's eye exactly seven weeks ago when he grabbed Edwin's translation notebook and discovered the hours Edwin had spent doodling in its margins. His pupils were flooded with curves and strange proportions, with double sets of eyes and sacred geometry. Leo and Edwin spent the rest of the afternoon together on the theater steps using stolen Walgreens markers to draw in the spaces that hadn't already been filled with Edwin's nightmares. I spent the rest of the afternoon on the same steps, feeling the tiles underneath me and my empty stomach, tracking the ebb and flow of their laughter. Leo didn't go to Readings from the Pacific that day; I didn't make it to Literary Theory.

If I'm honest, I don't know why I think I have any right to make a claim on Leo. One drunken night together doesn't justify my obsession, my footnotes on the page, the verses I've written with his salty aftertaste on my tongue. As it turns out, Leo likes to be touched when he's faded, falling all over the place, though we girls chalk it up to the hormones in the atmosphere, a certain horniness in the air. I remember one night in late July: we were celebrating Sarah's return from Granada, and the Bad Decisions

Club pooled some money to buy molly so pure that the tingling hit us in less than fifteen. We left behind dozens of Medalla cans, thirty-something cigarette packs, discarded bras, condom wrappers (thank god), empty baggies all over. We jumped to the sound of deep house from Berlin, until someone pulled up a reggaeton mix on YouTube with songs from the eleventh grade when the parties in the Caribe Hilton were flooded with blue smoke. Leo was shirtless and shaking his hips in the middle of the circle, a sweaty tangle of hair trailing from his chest to the top of his Calvin Kleins. I pinched his nipples because every once in a while I like to cause him pain, I live to hear him whimper. I tried to stimulate his asshole with my finger and I felt his hand wrap around my ass and squeeze. I turned up the look in my eyes to eleven and caught his attention. That night I licked my lips and let Yiyí in all her universal wisdom illuminate my path with her silver lightning bolts, allowing the universe to grant me a miracle just as I was beginning to lose faith in such things.

From time to time I get lucky. A few friends got too drunk and stayed the night at my place on Peregrina Street. Leo threw one of my pillows on the ground and was out like a light. My body throbbed from having him so close. I lay down too and pretended to sleep while my foot inched toward him. He didn't move. I persisted, emboldened by the bitter taste in my mouth and months of pent-up hormones that had taken over my dreams and my notebooks where I should have been conjugating the future subjunctive. Blessings like these don't come around often: I acknowledge them and move on to the next enigma. I never thought the thirst I had for his naked body could be quenched, not even by the waters that sprung the first signs of life billions of years ago. He is ancient moss. His body glistening with sweat, his warm, slow breath. I wait. Words can't express the feeling, nor describe his maw finally closing around my most trembling artic-ulations. I won't reduce it to words and extract it like the cancer it is: it belongs to me, to him, to the room where we existed as if time stood still.

One encounter was enough to stain all my words with his mystery. I have shaking fits because we breathe in the same time and space, because I let him share my friends and my hobbies and my blunts, now my bodily fluids.

I measure the hours of my day by counting the moments we're apart. I memorize his routes from building to building. I know exactly when to turn my head to see him wandering the halls between classes. I keep a record of which of Leo's doodles the janitors have yet to scrub off the bathroom stall. Sixty-three remain. What terrible disease is burning my lungs? Curse the time I drank from his waters, when eternity is the worst of all fates!

I dream Leo is drawing vines that reach up around Edwin's neck. He tattoos tiny orchids with teal stamens, ladybugs and hummingbirds sucking on their petals; their stems extend delicately across his rivers of blood, patches of black hair, between his baby-powdered thighs, in the spaces between his toes. I feel his fingers touch Edwin's skin as if they were my own; my hands graze his neck, drawing golden lines that bind us. I'm shaking from fear, disgusted by my soaked sheets. I run to the bathroom and expel a single mouthful of anxiety. I refuse to go out: I'd rather close all the windows and unplug the fan so I can sweat out the toxins in my body. I don't care what my friends say. They can pool their money and buy all the cigarettes and bottles of water they want, eat as much free food from the Pentecostals on Gándara Avenue as they please without me. Tonight I am held hostage by the shifting tides Leo's movements cause in my atmosphere—I'm trapped in his orbit, his dimensions multiply exponentially in my dreams. I'll stay in my room until I can learn to bear this repulsive condition: our overlap of time and space.

THEN THERE IS Edwin. I don't know where his body ends and my hunger for him begins. The idea of us falling in love crosses my mind. I see him look at me with that spark in his eye. A mutual yet inexpressible recognition of desire. He shares this fire with me, but perhaps it isn't fair to keep his flame all to myself. I don't know what to make of our chemistry, the effect he has on my biosphere, but Leo is starting to notice. Perhaps I should whisper things to Edwin, dirty things that I imagine only Leo is capable of doing to him, things that will make Edwin melt as my tongue moves in his ear. I try desperately to glue myself to his side, to be an essential member of our group chat, to invite him to lunch with me and Leo (or to insert myself and tag along when they try to sneak off and devour each other), to measure steps and smiles and anecdotes and Leo's little drawings as if they might become three-dimensional and leap from the page. I admit, at first my interest in Edwin was really a way to make Leo jealous that worked better than I'd anticipated, but Edwin can melt stars with his affections. Either that or I'm an idiot. One or the other.

I learn that Edwin is an amateur book collector. That he is a nomad with the eyes of a pirate and a Melquíades beard from another century slinging merchandise from a leather trunk. Some of his professors have even asked him for help getting rare books, and he always finds them. Edwin has been collecting them since freshman year, even though this year his enrollment was frozen because he didn't pay tuition on time, and that's why he has four months to kill and why Leo always has someone to distract himself with whenever his ADHD strikes. At first Edwin is just a way of spending time with Leo. I measure the hours with each of them by my side, feeling our contours and filling my mind with dreams that never become reality, with fantasies that keep me up half the night. But before long, an appreciation grows, a lightning bolt on the horizon, a late summer storm catching me by surprise. Before long I find myself thinking of Leo, of Edwin, of Leo and Edwin, of Edwin and then of Leo, of Edwin and I forget that Leo is on his way to meet us, but it's raining and we take shelter at the library until it passes, and I prefer to talk excitedly with Edwin about nineties cartoons and rediscover episodes from my childhood that I haven't thought about in forever. What an incredible skill he possesses! He manages to gain access to my most repressed memories, my night terrors from sixth grade, the bullying for being a little bitch in eighth grade. He thumbs through my blank pages and fills them with his mint-colored ink, departing with a kiss on the lips . . . and Leo pretends not to see us, passing a blunt on the theater steps with the others, but his laugh isn't very convincing.

That's why our clique is inseparable despite all the drama between us. Our love for weed takes precedence over Leo and Brian trading yaoi comics in August, or Brian professing his love for Edwin on the scraps of paper we use to clean up Marlboro ashes. The impulse to gather at the universally agreed-upon hour carries us through the months of torment Brian shared with Christian, the minidresses he would steal for him from Zara and Forever 21 that barely covered his ass, the ones Christian would lift up in the alley behind El Bori, when we all ignored the lipstick smeared on his neck and shoulders. The freedom to release blue smoke from my lungs takes precedence over the week in May I spent with Christian in my apartment when he was kicked out of his house and had an ocean of tears at his feet, and we fucked for five days and I cooked him rice with chicken stuffed with sweet plantains, because the incessant rain kept us in bed, in the kitchen, in the shower, on the balcony. The promise of another blunt convinces me to get together with Madéline, just after Leo had told her to go to hell and I was the only one who responded to her texts, and she had no way to thank me except with the gyration of her hips. A polyhedron of regret and denial has accumulated vertices between us, but the months pass and the ashes keep falling, and the butterflies in my stomach take me back to the sweetness of being seven. We block the sun with our thumbs and bind ourselves with threads of spit, like fractals floating adrift.

Edwin draws caricatures of me. I find them in my Portuguese notebook. He draws me with dark sunglasses, smoking a blunt. The smoke wraps around my clumsy sentences, and a pale-pink orchid (the only color against the black and white) rests on my cheek, giving my face a strange softness. I run to the bathroom. He couldn't have possibly recognized me—seen the part of me the mirror has never reflected. I look at my infinite reflections, pulsing with his existence, his heat, my coldness. I see myself through another, through his black-hole eyes that suck me in, and his lines that dreamed me into another creature. For the first time in months, I stop shaking and the cold dissipates; my stomach rumbles with hunger instead of pure anxiety. I recite poems for him that are never written down. Verses that rock in his wake and then splash in toilet bowls, verses of thanks for having returned me to my body, verses I'll take to my grave.

SOMETIMES I DON'T understand Leo's spell over me. Maybe it's the way he debates our national history with our other friends, with a calmness that wraps around us like smoke (so different from me), an amateur percussionist slapping his body to improvise rhymes that I jot down on random street corners. Perhaps it's his taste for Catalan punk, his anarchism, his inclination toward queer communism, his crooked left canine, twisted just so. Perhaps it's his tendency to expel bodily gases and blow them in my direction. Perhaps it's his way of turning down every attempt I make at repeating that scene from our first season on *The Real World: San Juan*.

The worst part is not being able to tell anyone about it. People go on and on about their fantasies of fucking their cousins, or the hetero-reproductivity that dominates our culture, or the person they met on Grindr that they kicked out of bed because they're psycho or because they shaved their pubes. Sometimes I ask myself how I ended up in this group chat, with people that send photos of trips to Isabela with molly under their tongues or snorting lines of coke off their iPhones, videos of René dancing at the La Dieciocho bus stop wearing a Julia de Burgos mask, videos of Carlos snoring in the library an hour before his physics exam. An update of our lives every fifteen minutes. The alerts I can't ignore even when they're on vibrate, the threads that yank me from my shadows and wrap around the pillars of the theater steps, pulling at our leg hairs, translating our time together into memes.

We're doomed to be in the same classes

with the same fucking professors, to take refuge in the theater when it suddenly starts to rain. And I'm doomed to watch Leo and Edwin falling in love in front of my eyes, reading aloud from the anonymous love notes I stick in their notebooks. I try to enjoy the suffering, to walk steadily through the heat of a nuclear sun, to allow my stomach to contract because it means pounds lost and days without dirtying a single plate. Hands held, half kisses while resting their heads on their books—no one comments on my face turning the color of a bruise, or my body's quiet rattle. I have no one to vent to. I'm not one to talk about my internal turmoil. I'd rather keep it to myself, throw myself face down on the tiled steps and map out the ashes, write Leo and Edwin off with the stroke of a pen, wish them decades of mediocre love and STDs and nights reeling through galaxies. The emerald lizard stares at me and sheds its skin: I guess karma is handed out in ways I'll never understand.

It's weird: Leo plays dumb, like he'd rather spare my feelings and our friendship than acknowledge the imbalance between us. Sometimes I'd prefer he tell me to leave him the fuck alone, send me away, abandon me with little pieces of my brain sliding down the wall, let me drag myself into some dark hole to lick my wounds the way I always have. That's how I recover when I get rejected for a scholarship, when I fail a Portuguese exam, when my grandfather dies and I have no choice but to lock myself in my room for weeks without any contact with the outside world other than my grandmother knocking on the door to let me know the sausage and rice she left me is getting cold.

On Monday we meet for dollar-beer night at El Refu. Sure, Olga has a Humanities exam and Madéline has a US History paper due and I have a presentation on Andrés Caicedo to finish. But we plan to drop acid the week after next at Gilligan's Island because the school decided to issue the last scholarship check right before a long weekend. Camila gives me a ride and picks up Leo on the way (who is with Edwin, surprise surprise). We run toward an empty table because it starts to rain and just as the flying cockroaches descend on the pizza empanadillas Leo appears next to me with his last dollar bill covering his face. He asks me to spot him, he'll pay me back. I tell him I don't want his money, that what I want is a bottle of water. He says please. With my eyes I reply that he's got no idea how long I've been waiting to hear him beg.

I tell Vero I left my weed in the car and she tosses me the keys to her Montero. Leo comes with me and we count the doses of ecstasy we took over Halloween weekend. He lifts up his arm and sniffs his armpit and asks me if he should wear more deodorant, but I'm an idiot and don't smell him even though my guts are already twisting with hunger. We get in the car and I grab my bowl and pack it as fast as I can and Leo laughs and I pretend to laugh too and I pull at the hair on his legs and he tells me to stop and I tell him that we should economize the weed and that's why we should pass the smoke we inhale from mouth to mouth and I grab him by the neck and his eyes open wide and I measure the desperation in his face and in my mouth and understand that they don't match up; the smoke leaves my lungs into the stale car before I can contain it. My desire multiplies with his gasp of shock at seeing me suddenly so close to him. Maybe he hasn't had enough fifths of rum to drink . . . but I tell him I want him, that sometimes I can't or don't want to control myself. He says I should pay more attention to the way he ignores all my attempts. I tell him that most of the time I feel things I don't want to feel, I can't help it, it's my nature. Leo says he doesn't know what to say. He gets out of the car, I buy a bottle of water, and we join in with everyone else's laughter like I haven't just been reduced to a pile of shit at Leo's feet.

THE MESSAGE COMES through and I reply. They want me to buy weed for them. Of course I respond. Of course I'll get some. Come to my apartment, run. Of course they arrive in five minutes.

Leo kisses me on the cheek like nothing happened the night before. Edwin doesn't mention the poem I left in his bag during lunch and kisses the same cheek. We sit down to watch episodes of *Dragon Ball Z*, the Buu Saga, and can't believe such badass creatures exist. We note that when they transform into Super Saiyan, they're really just flexing and posing for each other. Vegeta just wants to fuck Goku, but won't because he thinks he's too macho, and he would try getting fucked in the ass if he weren't so afraid of liking it. We laugh because we haven't watched this show since we were kids, and it's not the same after taking so many gender studies classes. I'm thankful for my education and its inherent liberation, Leo laments the death of our childhood innocence, and Edwin starts packing the bowl. We've locked ourselves in together for hours.

It's time for a nail-polish party. Leo laughs at us for being such queens. Edwin laughs at the color he chooses. I laugh at the pain of having them so close to me and yet so far away: the three of us on the couch. Leo with his head on Edwin's lap while I try to caress his nipple. We disagree about the best way to cook a chicken breast. I suggest he bake it at three hundred and seventy-five degrees for thirty minutes or until golden brown. I look at our reflection in the mirror on the wall and see something that could work, a blurry but discernible future taking shape between the three of us like danger, a possibility that stretches out in front of us like an erection. We decide to paint our toes bright red, mint green, metallic gold. But first we clean off our old polish, dipping our fingers into a container of acetone-drenched foam with a hole in the center. I recognize the feeling of pressure around my index finger. Edwin says it looks like a sphincter. Leo doesn't say anything, instead he pulls us in for a kiss that knocks over the acetone and we throw ourselves on the couch to bathe the cushions in spit. Something in my body comes to life and I start weeping tears of joy. The strange thing is, Edwin also starts crying. Then Leo. It's hot so we strip down. Then it starts to rain. The breeze it brings carries us, and we don't want to be doing anything else, aren't capable of doing anything else, can't believe we are touching one another in the same time and space, so intimately and with so much yet to be discovered, with the new lines we draw between planets, with their mysteries and mine, with my secrets and theirs, with all the built-up desires and matter endlessly imploding. I see myself in their faces, and they see themselves in mine, though the measurements aren't quite the same and the angles are more obtuse. Today I want time to stop. I don't care if the universe doesn't stop with us, or if our alarms keep going off before we're ready to get up: one of six hands will reach over and shut them off.

Now all we have to do is open our eyes, find one another now that the fantasy has passed, and decide the trajectory of the rest of our lives. The chat vibrates on the nightstand, the sun rises a silvery blue, and I never want to be without them. I think it would hurt less to sew our kidneys together and urinate through the same orifice. Leo sighs and Edwin stretches his arms over his head. The shakes come on slowly, rising from my red fingernails. I'm consumed by vertigo, and I don't know whether it's because I'm hungry or desperate.

We don't know what to do with all the hours that lie ahead.

In the Bathhouse

AFTER MANUEL RAMOS OTERO

> "Alienation, however, does not lead our hero out
> of society, but deeper into it, for he is impelled by
> a curiosity to know, down to the smallest detail,
> the corrupt world that he wishes to escape."
> —LARRY KRAMER, *FAGGOTS*

I'm a dumbass. And I'll do my part on this island filling it up with other dumbasses like me. With rich people side-eyeing me at every red light. With locas who just came out of the closet and haven't learned how to protect themselves yet. With Angélica. I'm a dumbass because I work at a clinic administering rapid HIV tests in a country where people refuse to get tested. Whether the results take fifteen minutes or three days, it doesn't matter. No. I could care less about finding a cure. Why? Because diseases like HIV, like cancer, like the flu, serve to control overpopulation—all the excess people who are going to turn the world into a burned-out hunk of charcoal. A cure doesn't interest me because I tested positive at twenty and I already know I won't find love—the only cure I need, the only reason to want to go on living. I'm going to die at twenty-seven with a used-up smile. I also work nights at the bathhouse on Parada 22, Wednesday through Friday, right near my day job on Eduardo Conde. I pop in my headphones and listen to Madonna (the *Like a Prayer* era, never the *MDNA* era) while I walk down the hill, ring the doorbell, step through the blue light, climb the dark stairs, undress, and then work eight straight hours in a thong I own in *shocking pink*, in *chartreuse green*, in *cherry jubilée* . . . Whatever: the point is I show off my fat ass, which I've been self-conscious about since the ninth grade but the guys with the biggest dicks seem to like it. Who knows. The meds make me drop weight like a candle melting on an altar in front of a saint . . . In the middle of the night, I fearlessly walk the mazelike streets of Santurce because violence is like seroconversion: you can avoid it all you want but it's gonna happen. You can try to gain a little control over how and when. The most beautiful and brutal things in this life happen like that: suddenly, terribly, cathartically.

I'VE ALWAYS BEEN strange. I care about things no one else cares about. The inverse is also true. I care about having a fresh gallon of milk in the fridge. I don't care about remembering (or even knowing, for that matter) the names of the men I sleep with. I care about getting a front-row seat in my Puerto Rican art lecture (because the professor is eighty years old and the sound of his voice transports me and because the weed makes me imagine every painting he describes as surrealist). I don't care about air-conditioning. I care about white rice. I don't care about the meaning of life. I care about masturbation. I don't care about small children. I care about the liberation of Puerto Rico. I don't care about love. But then, I do. Then again, I couldn't give a shit. Love just lands. You don't look for it. It tethers itself to your body and drags you away like a comet hurtling through the night. You don't look for love, because it can't be found. If I looked for love the way I look for dick, pieces of my heart would end up in every library urinal. In every mangrove of the Capital and around Boquerón. To be honest, sometimes I feel broken into a million pieces anyway. Memories of me spread against walls with perverts asking to be jerked off and stepped on, memories written in cum that I clean off the bathroom floor and then watch spiral down the toilet, memories of the patio of my grandmother's house, La Concha stairs, Mar Chiquita reefs, Condado beach. Yes, I'm a bathroom regular. So what? I love to feel my balls contract when some stranger peeks through the crack in the stall door and sees my erection in my left hand, then goes to the neighboring stall and starts jerking off (I will be forever grateful to the Adam who had the idea of drilling a hole in the wall, eye level with someone squatting like a crow on the toilet seat, at just the right height for them to see you playing with your foreskin). My mouth waters just at the thought of it. It also disgusts me.

I DON'T CARE about prevention because I got infected right from the beginning. Right from the very first breeding at seventeen. That's what I suspect anyway ... To be honest I don't really know who infected me, but whoever it was I'm sure was cured in the act. He took the purest part of my being, the virginity that transcended any sexual act. That's why I'm a dumbass. Because I let it happen and delighted in my metamorphosis. I suppose it was probably the soldier from Aguadilla who came all the way to San Juan when I told him I had the house to myself. I told him to hurry because the rain was chilling my bones, and warm like the summer sun he pulled me onto his big dick and tore up my ass for two hours until he screamed and then the sound of him snoring resounded through the empty house. He filled me with his sweat and cum. He lit my insides on fire. I can still feel the original big bang and the residual hot ash that burns red despite having been passed from one generation to the next—the radioactive material he used to make me sick, me and all the people around me. Then I fucked him and came inside him, like an idiot. The next day, when I went out to fuck for the second time (because when I get the craving there is no way to shake it), I fucked an athlete on a scholarship from Río Piedras with caramel skin and a fat ass. I don't like the feeling of a condom, so I ripped it off and kept fucking him. I came inside him too. They never complain. They almost never complain. It makes me feel free, sometimes. It also makes me a dumbass.

AT THE CLINIC I collect souls. I have direct access to social-security numbers and credit cards . . . I wouldn't ever do anything with them, but it's tempting. Who knows. I always ask the same questions and get the same answers. Yes, they've been tested. Yes, they use drugs: weed, coke, dope, molly, speed, a little bit of everything, like salad. Yes, they are at risk, that's why they sit two feet from my pen with that look of terror in their eyes. Yes, they are afraid—I can tell by that prehistoric stench. With my eyes I communicate that I under-stand them, that I knew their results as soon as they walked in, that I'm happy about it. That's how you learn, dumbass. That's how it is. That's how our animal instincts develop. Just like that, with one fuck (only one, or hundreds, or thousands), you toss your life into the void. Because that's life: constant death. Sex isn't life, it's a death: the most minuscule death, la petite mort. I die multiple times per day. They murder me, atrociously, with bullet wounds and stabbings, multiple times a day. Some-times I murder myself with tenderness, with rage, with haste. Sometimes I want to murder in cold blood, to make someone else suffer, to set the deterioration of a body in motion so that in ten years it rots and disintegrates like a dried-up fetus in a belly, and break the cycle. It's not that I'm horny: I'm suicidal. Sometimes I cry thinking about the past and about dangerous things, and I sit down in the shower with the water as hot as it goes and my skin glows red like the setting sun.

MY UNIVERSITY MAKES me sad. So many abandoned buildings (more than you might expect), so much free time to sit and smoke in the Humanities buildings while blowing off your French homework. There are a lot of people I'd like to say hi to but they avoid eye contact. I waited so long to enroll in classes for next semester that I missed the deadline. I'm a dumbass for leaving it till the last minute, and I don't know anyone in administration to offer sexual favors to. In my mind I repeat to myself that I am a scholar, that I am going to be a professor of queer Puerto Rican literature. Then I remember I'm going to die at twenty-seven in an assault, murdered by a lowlife drug addict, and before long I'm back on my bullshit—horny in my favorite library bathroom stall waiting for the next customer to come in. It's always the same ones—a DOE secretary, a bartender from the main strip, an unemployed social worker—and they think I can't identify which cumshot corresponds to which dick. Eventually I get tired and jerk off a few times while listening to Cultura Profética (but from *Diario*, never from *La Dulzura*) to kill some time before my shift at the bathhouse starts. As I arrive my stress lowers. Here I know my role. Muscle memory. Greet the regular clients with a wink, collect their IDs, give them a key to a locker or to a room. I rub the dirty towels on my face, absorbing the musk of wet male, and then let them fall from my arms into the washing machine. I disregard the instructions to wear plastic gloves to pick up the used condoms off the floor. No one notices, because no one pays me any mind. Not because I am unattractive, but because they're busy. There is no pool or gym or even a clean surface to sit down on. If they aren't fucking, they are frustrated and pacing around in circles watching other people fuck. The best days are Saturdays, when the cars line up along Fernández Juncos Avenue and the bathhouse fills to capacity, when men bounce off the corrugated metal walls like comets, when you can hear doors opening and closing all night, when the sound of the neon-lit showers fails to drown out the moans and grunts and I dissolve into the crowd. For the record, my favorite days are Thursdays, when there's no cover for customers under twenty-one and I blast Lady Gaga (from *Born This Way*, even though I don't even really like that album) and turn off the lights.

Sometimes I think love will find me at the bathhouse, but at most I'll probably just confuse it for a good fuck. Despite my supposed wisdom, I still haven't felt the intimacy of a loving relationship—not even from my mother, who abandoned me at my grandparents' house and ran away to Orlando, or from my father, who had a string of kids along the southern coast. So I've come to the conclusion that love doesn't actually exist—or maybe it does? Maybe I've felt it, for real, outside a momentary hormonal flash? No, I know better. Love is just a perfect illusion that escapes all reason. I'd like to think we're beyond these mind games, that we're no longer capable of giving ourselves over to one another like the sun and moon surrendering themselves to the inevitability of an eclipse. I reject centuries of machismo and closetry. I recuse myself from finding love with creepy old men who think they're hot shit cruising in the dark, or with potbellied bears who can't get laid so they brush up against you, or anyone, for a rush, or with married guys who forget to take off their wedding rings. I think I could be happy somewhere else, on another island. If I ever fall in love completely, it won't be with a Puerto Rican. Never. If my people are incapable of seeing beyond themselves, how can they feel true love? I'd prefer to die at twenty-seven at the hand of a crazy junky who throws me over the De Diego guardrail into the whirring traffic of the Baldorioty Expressway. That's why I'm moving to New York. Soon. Somehow, some-way. In fact, it's long overdue. I want to live the life of a go-go dancer in a gay club. In La Escuelita. In the Greenhouse. In Splash. In the Boiler Room.

Even though I'm going to die at twenty-seven in one of the gun fights that happen every Thursday night near Vidy's, I'd prefer to prolong the inevitable for as long as I can. Long, but not so long that I disappear like an

extinguished star succumbing to a black sky:
I want to be a celestial flare, a red giant burst-
ing in a macrocosmic blaze, dragging all who
wish along in my fiery trail. I want to play my
part in the extinction of the species. To contrib-
ute to the statistics, to the federally funded
projects, to the isolation. Here we crash into
one another. And I'm tired of this putrid little
island, of my ocean view and the traffic jams
on the freeway. I'm tormented by those flashing turquoise and scarlet lamplights the locas
from Sacred Heart University ignore. I'm sick
of working, sick of these empty hours. Sometimes I think the gringos live better than we
do, except they don't know how to appreci-
ate the flavor Blackness leaves in your mouth.
They can't know how delicious tight curly hair
is, almond eyes, heavy dicks. In New York there
are plenty of Black people, plenty of Domini-
cans too. I'm craving plantains . . . Maybe today
I'll make tostones.

I apologize—it's just that I'm on my fourth
blunt and I'm in my own world. Lately the weed
I buy comes from Colorado and I get greedy.
I'm going to die at twenty-seven from pneu-
monia that I'll ignore; that's why I need my

natural medicine starting now. Botanical. But I'm not one of those people who think they live in a beer commercial either, I swear I'm not like that. I don't chill twenty-four-seven. Though I'm sure that, since I was raised to be a good Christian boy, if this very morning someone were to ask me how I'm doing, I would tell them great! Better than ever. Super. Trés bien. I wouldn't tell them I couldn't eat breakfast because nausea and diarrhea turned my intestines to liquid. I wouldn't mention the new blotch on my dorsal spine. I wouldn't tell them I need to go to the clinic today so I don't run out of meds; that if I skip even just for one day, I'll spoil months of consistency; that if I skip even just for an hour, my body will start to go to shit; that if I wait another minute, I will shit myself from anxiety and need to be taken to the hospital and die from shame. But today I'm cold and don't feel like taking the train, and there is an asteroid field tearing my insides to shreds.

Fucking pills. They destroy me from the inside out. They give me night terrors. They give me bloodcurdling dreams. They make me piss the bed like I did when I was seven years old. If

I just learn to stop the nightmares, I can break the cycle. Sometimes I dream that red ants are eating my dick with molten-hot steel clamps for mouths. Sometimes I dream that I'm being dismembered and chopped into tiny pieces at twenty-seven, a victim of a hate crime, dragged from Loíza to Río Grande without ever finding love. Sometimes whole days flash before my eyes—classes, traffic jams, hunger, sex, coffee, water, weed—and when I blink, I realize I'm still in bed, thinking I'm alive when I'm not, aging twenty-four hours in twenty-four seconds. Some nights I don't sleep at all. Some mornings I can hardly lift my head up off the pillow.

After my shift at the bathhouse I walk the Santurce streets to feel alone. I walk from Del Parque Street to Miramar and stop at Olimpo to absorb the first morning light. I pop in my headphones and listen to Amy Winehouse (from *Frank*, not *Back to Black*) because I very much identify with her lyrics. The early morning sky turns cloudy and the shadows stretch long as the sun comes up. San Juan looks abandoned. I see myself in everything. I'm the junky gringo with a blond beard who sleeps in a bank doorway and dreams of his former banker life. I'm the old textile factory that's been reduced to rubble. I'm the queen limping around Condado unable to find customers because her sores smear her purple lipstick. I am the avenue. I am everything that glimmers in the last shadows of night. The glass shards, used syringes, broken car windows. I'm surrounded by fallen stars and the hunger returns to me. I want to suck dick. But the runners are all the way on Ashford, and I don't have the strength to walk there let alone convince someone to pull their pants down for me. Now I must be dreaming because the graffiti peels itself off the buildings, the rust-colored giraffes with twisted necks stampede, trampling drunk drivers, obsidian lizards with granite eyes drag their tongues and taste the dirty street, and I'm just a hooded figure with a vulture's face, dressed in black, shrinking in the rain between asbestos-ridden buildings. Then I come to. I am in my room covered in white with a brush and a tube of paint and am not sure whether I'm the one who's been painting white crosses on the streets or, on the contrary, that miserable faggot always escaping and insisting on defacing the walls.

I've come to the conclusion that I do not exist. I am. I am not. I don't know what I am, I am something . . . I am a dumbass because I'm still in bed. I don't have the courage to open my eyes and find myself still in kindergarten with my hand down Alexander's pants, and learn that all these years were just a hallucination, the kind only children can see. I'm an infant, I know. I still don't know how to speak. I still don't know how to walk. I don't know how I managed to get this second job . . . maybe because the owner says I suck dick better than anyone.

A disturbing pattern has emerged. Both of my jobs essentially are the same: I give out condoms, promote prevention—but don't ask me how many I've given out in the six months I've worked there. Some nights at least a hundred men come and go, but I can count on one hand the times I've refilled the condom bucket. Just before dawn, when there are no more keys to hand out and it stops raining wet towels, I walk home to my apartment. The truth is I'm not afraid. I know what to expect as I walk down Sagrado Corazón Avenue. To feel more alone than ever. For even my shadow to abandon me and escape down the dark streets. It doesn't seem like anyone lives in these houses. They've already turned to ghosts lighting lamps in the night. There's no breeze at all, toujours. I choke with loneliness. I would walk up Bouret Street, but a Black guy and his two lovers live there and they make fun of me when I walk by, and I yell "Ay, qué rico" so they don't realize I'm a dumbass, but they laugh with fiery breath and say, "Awww come on, don't be like that, don't be like that."

I gave out tests for two years before I took one when I was closing up the office one day. I turned out the lights and pricked myself three times to be sure. The lines appeared on all three tests. I didn't have support from anyone and didn't need it anyway. I let out a sigh of relief. I cried tears of joy. I don't have to be anxious for the rest of my life, busying myself to delay the inevitable. Now I will take Atripla once daily and my problems will be resolved. That's how I will break the cycle—by entering into another. Now I only fuck at night so no one will say a word to me, so they hear me open the condom but don't see me "put it on." I hear them moan when my dick slips inside them and their balls get hot with pleasure. Biological. If they put it on for me, well fine, I'll play along even though I can't keep it up as easily. But that hardly ever happens. You wouldn't believe how rarely they ask about my status. Or how easily I lie. Très facile. Sure, I took the test on June 27, the so-called National HIV Testing Day, and I arrived just as they were closing and the fat Black guy who worked there gave it to me anyway. He gave me the results after fifteen minutes: negative. When I say it, I look them in the eyes with a naughty smile and they eat it up. Is it really that easy? Of course it is. I've already given that speech three times today. Next time I'll change it up, keep it fresh.

That gets me thinking about something I've always said: I love my island, but I hate the people. No one here is worth a damn. Nothing is worth shit anymore . . . How things change. Some changes are irreversible and we can't escape the rattling in our bones. Like death. Like a virus. Like sex. My world is a spinning top falling through space, and Puerto Rico sold its soul to tourism. I don't deal well with the cold, I start to shiver, but I still wake up drenched in sweat. That's why I keep going back to the bathhouse: to bring my temperature down to absolute zero and kneel down in a stall to wait for a faceless hand to offer its warmth, rub my dick like firewood, spark an explosion that stretches across a black-hole abyss, an orgasmic supernova that reheats my body like a belly-up lizard on a rock at noon. Come to think of it, just the other day I reconnected with a nurse from Centro Médico whom I'd crossed paths with at a motel near Aguadilla. One of my many excursions that month. Back in Río Piedras I get a Grindr message that he's on campus, and I go to meet him, even though I was headed toward Jesús T. Piñero Avenue. We go to the fourth-floor bathroom of the Business Administration building and into one of the stalls. With his dick in my mouth, I stick a finger in his ass before he turns around and hands me a condom (thank god he has a Magnum). I don't tell him anything because he doesn't ask, nor does he turn around to look and make sure. He cums and I feel an unfamiliar urge to smile. For some reason, while we wash our hands, I hug him. There's no hint of rejection in his eyes. The smell of his pink polo is intoxicating; his torso is soft, slightly deflated. I watch him observe my hands slide along his forearms and neither of us wants to let go. I'm afraid if I speak the moment might shatter. We're still for almost fifteen minutes, floating.

"Does this feel weird for you?"

"Super weird."

"Ah, okay . . . Should I stop?"

"No, no . . . I don't mean it like that. I just wasn't expecting it, but I like it."

"Chemical."

I could tell he was breathtaking when he was younger. His name is Omar. Omar. Now I can say I fell in love with an Omar in the bathroom of the University of Puerto Rico. C'est magnifique . . . but he woke something that had died in me. I want to see my reflection in his eyes while I breed him with the burning feeling in my belly. I want to feel myself on top of him, wrapping around him, without a condom to separate our love, to feel that with one fuck I could close the cycle and be born again. I want to stop hunting down dick like a vampire, but like everything in this life (like everything on this island), I find it impossible to do. So now I ignore his texts. Now he doesn't exist. He's just more graffiti marking my city's walls. I dream of men like him from time to time. That's why

I'm a dumbass, because I just drift along, let the current take me and drag me under . . . C'est la vie.

It's not sustainable to test negative or positive every morning and then go to the bathhouse the same night. It's a push and pull that gives me whiplash; I see the same faces over and over in contrasting spaces. Maybe my brain is just fried from all the pills. I've been smoking a lot of crystal lately. I can concentrate but don't sleep for three days straight, and I enter a new plane of consciousness. I see a lot of monsters. When I cum, I cum drops of dawn. They never ask me for condoms, but they always request clean towels. Lube, yes. They ask me for a lot of lube, and it costs them two dollars extra. Apparently friction is more important than self-preservation. People want to die, that's the thing. I'm a dumbass for wanting to help people who don't want to be helped. Protection isn't enough. Motivation isn't enough. There's something in the water or in the air or in the heat that makes us dig our own graves, then climb into them and wait for hurricane season, for water to cleanse us, submerge us, drown us. Then stagnate. This is my personal glory hole.

Welcome. Remember, clothing is prohibited. A towel around the waist or nothing. Lingerie optionnelle.

I have to tell myself the universe will eventually return itself to equilibrium. Ce sont les lois de la physique. Everything returns to ash, and when it's your turn to die, the same sun you were born under keeps rising. Life is tedious, an aimless dream that never ends. It's only when I close my eyes that I truly am, and so with death I wake. This world has stopped making sense. There's no rhyme or reason: the purest of us wind up dead in a gutter bled dry and soulless, the filthiest remain with the marrow of the stars, and everyone in between surrenders to entropy. It's absurd. I'd rather die open-mouthed while fucking at the age of twenty-seven. When I go all my deaths will flash by me in one macabre flow of consciousness: burnt at the stake and vomiting demons in a nameless, timeless forest and watching a tribe push a giant fireball out the mouth of an erupting volcano. That's how I'll break the cycle. I've been told I'm like a train gone off the rails. It's just as well.

Meanwhile I get ready for another shift.

I take my pills—hardly paying attention to which is which. It's already getting late. I crawl into a crepuscular world. It's the last Saturday of the month and the owner lets me be the star of the show. I shaved my head for the occasion. I don't want to look human. I want to look like something else entirely. I'm another species and at the same time, I'm not. People around me notice: I can tell by the way they look at me. I'm their mirror: most would kill to be in my place. The other star arrives, an ex-lover, a Black photographer with a kilometric dick. We undress (except for my bright-red jockstrap) on the improvised stage near the lockers. I start kissing him with a lot of tongue and the clients gather round. They look like little nocturnal monsters with their big eyes, with the red glow on their eyelids, watching us. He opens a pack of condoms, but I whisper in his ear that we don't need one, that I'm clean, and he smiles and pulls me against him. I begin to leave my body when his nails dig into my hips. I hear panting all around me. I become the vapor that fogs up the porn playing on the TV screens. More dicks come, more faceless bodies. I'm a virus traveling from mouth to mouth. I yell something I once read in a Humanities bath-room stall: "Don't pull out, leave it inside! Fill my ass with cum!" I turn into hot, milky seed on the bathroom floor. I feel vibration and heat deep in my ass. I'm just another body in a dark room that stinks of sweat. I climb into the middle and get fucked by several different people, mercilessly, without ever needing to look behind me. They cover me with their junk. They cover the biohazard tattoo just above my ass; it melts under the scarlet light and grunts like a skull. I turn into something that exists, doesn't exist, an entity that dies at twenty-seven because they've always been, at the very core, a dumbass. That's how I transcend my own skin and get out. I'm a dumbass because it's easier that way. I'm a dumbass because I'm an Aries and I like to play with fire.

Helium

I'm not one to take Valentine's Day seriously. But my mother has always been the complete opposite—we are the typical mother and son who refuse to see eye to eye, who refuse to share secrets and greet each other with a kiss on the cheek. And it's not that I don't like my mother . . . There's just this longstanding iciness floating in the air between us, making any exchange echo like howls deep in a frozen forest. It is an ancient separation, omnipresent, that stretches out from her eyes and into mine, encasing us in silence. Maybe it's because I was never breastfed: my mother contracted some wicked bacteria from the C-section, and we never bonded during those crucial first days. And so I seethed on my grandmother's bosom while some unpronounceable intruder attacked my mother's kidneys and threatened mine.

Every year my mother cashes her paycheck on Valentine's Day, if not the day before. Since I was in preschool, she's tried to cross our wall of silence by way of discounted sweet nothings in Walgreens's holiday aisle. She's nothing if not consistent: On Valentine's she wakes up two hours earlier than usual, shakes me awake from another night of sleeplessness, and forces my head and arms into crimson Tweety sweaters. She pulls at my scalp with her own hairbrush, scraping at the dead skin cells and tangling her dead hairs with mine. She asks me to make myself a sandwich because her hands are trembling from the latest weeklong diet-pill binge, even though I'm just five years old and have to climb onto the stove to reach the cupboards. While I make do with whatever my grandmother left in the fridge the week before, my mother teases and curls her auburn halo, colors her lips with bloody lipstick and fuchsia lip liner, pinches her cheeks, and dons some crazy heart-printed blouse that she buys, year after year, one size too small. "Love is in the air," she says while I choke down a mayonnaise and peanut butter and raw egg sandwich, and she squeezes herself into scarlet leggings and leaves a heart-shaped lip print on the mirror, further damaging her already deranged smile. Then I return to the kitchen and start on days' worth of dishes.

Then I wait . . . The surprise always shows up sooner or later. She goes all out during her lunch break with Snoopy and Woodstock balloons, Hallmark phrases drawn in my notebooks with i's dotted with hearts, and the teachers sigh throughout nap time. She buys industrial-sized bags of Snickers, Twix, KitKat, and Crunch bars for the Cupid-winged teaching assistants, who throw handfuls into the air for the children to catch with their mouths. My mother watches through the window, but she never sees how I hide from her, dodging the feast of candy. I skirt the room until I'm underneath the window she's looking through. I melt into the wall. Some years I bite into the balloons and inhale deeply, reading her notes to myself out loud until the helium makes me pass out and the teachers have to pull the nap mat from under me. Other times I just stare at the beaming, heart-shaped faces and smiles, sucking on my thumb with fury.

After Valentine's we have no milk in the fridge for a week. In the weeks after the holiday, teachers write in my red notebooks asking my mother to explain why I've developed dark circles under my eyes and why I end up treating the other children's mothers with icy disdain, why I cry when they come to pick up my classmates while I always have to wait until five, sometimes later. I play with blocks in a corner while I wait, wondering what it would be like to sleep warm and not locked inside an air-conditioned closet of a room. When I can read and write well enough, I quickly master her handwriting and learn to answer my teachers' prying questions with bright-red ink and hearts over the i's and bloody kisses printed over the words I have trouble spelling. That way they never suspect how my mother locks herself in her room the rest of February, sometimes until the end of March, stealing the chocolates she showered me with on the fourteenth and stockpiling them into the cellulite on her thighs and underarms. Recognizing the signs, my grandmother stays with us for weeks, bringing her prayer groups to meet in our dim living room, filling the house with cinnamon and sandalwood, praying for the patron saint of love and marriage to bless our home. Their visits always seem more mournful than they should. I hide in my room so I don't turn to stone when my mother finally snaps and crash-opens her door, screaming at them to keep the praying down. My grandmother flies back to Florida until the next year, and my mother triple-locks herself back in her room.

And again, no fresh food in the fridge, not even chocolates to stave off the hunger.

My grandmother passed away a few years ago, right before I turned fourteen. I've stopped trying to reach my mother from outside of her room, scratching at the door like some hungry lapdog, begging for Mommy to shoo away the winged baby with glowing ruby eyes glittering in my room night after night, filling my dreams with helium. Sometimes I picture her still waiting by her bedroom door, holding her ear against the wood, praying soundlessly for me to break her out of her stupor. One year she couldn't cry as silently and let one gasp slip out, a baby's whisper, I think, and I'm so shocked by the sound that I run to my room while she searches the whole house for me. She gives up and returns to her room without complaint, but eventually she finds me fake-snoring under the covers and forgets to kiss me goodnight. Nowadays I just check my Facebook and scoff at the couples posting pictures of their first-ever

Valentine's Day together, sipping champagne and diving into chocolate fondue, wearing expensive Marshalls suits and plunging scarlet dresses. Stoned on the couch, stuffing my face with Reese's and staring at my phone for hours, I post pictures of these dates, blowing up their dates' awkward, barely hidden boners pressing out of their pants. I can't wait for this year's parade of desperation, my chance to call them all out, and bask in the irony of so much romance and performance that I can only read as scantily veiled indifference.

This year, my mother has a boyfriend. I never find out until it's too late for me to do anything about it, before I've had a chance to neutralize any threats to our precarious stability. Not that I care, anyway. We still rarely see each other: I go to school while she works most nights at the gas station peddling condoms to sex workers and fake marijuana to parolees, saving up for that weekend trip she'll take this year on Valentine's. This year, I can honestly say she's going all out: she's booked a three-night getaway near the southern coast where there are dolphins from dawn to dusk—according to the page I unearth in her search history. She packs her bags and lets them sit out in the living room all night, as if to mock me. She buys strong rose-scented perfume and pink champagne and human-sized teddy bears. She even snags a heart-shaped pie with Nutella and almonds and a fresh-strawberry border. I almost destroy the damn pie because I come home famished after school and she forbids me to take a slice. She communicates this to me via a Post-it she leaves on the box. I flip the Post-it the bird and go lock myself in my room, where I find her gifts on my bed: a fresh carpet of Hershey's almond Kisses, substitutes for the real thing.

I should ask her what her boyfriend's name is, but I actually care so little what he calls himself. He could have a decent job, but would that mean he's compatible with my mother? I don't even know if I'm a good match for her as a son. I mean, Valentine's Day is just another day of the month, right? I'd rather not care at all, so I just lounge on my bed with death metal blaring from my speakers, cover the floor with foil wrappers, bite into my balloons and breathe out the helium, wondering why the hell I've been crying for so long.

Then I sit by the door, waiting for a frigid thrill to sneak in underneath. I can feel body heat on the other side; it's my mother, also crying silently. I can tell: the door trembles just so, and the tinny slams ricochet off the walls in my room despite the air-conditioning and the icy stalactites forming under my nostrils. I check my phone and it's already past ten, already way past the time her boyfriend should have picked her up—and then I realize why she's crying, why I'm crying, why we're so ashamed by that deafening frozen landscape between us that we can't just knock on the door and cross that infinite void and break the silence. But I can't fix the years of instability, can't make her any less lonely nor this day any more special than any other, and she can't take back all those days she wasted behind a locked door alone, leaving me out here crying.

Maybe this year I should stay up with her and descend into my own bell jar, fester in my own pool of silence. Or maybe I should go to Walgreens and buy her a gift. But I simply don't understand these mechanics, these yearly rituals of love. I can't condense so deep a feeling into a twenty-dollar budget. I can't open the door and take her to dinner, brave an hour of small talk and really face her, melt all those icy years keeping us apart. I wouldn't know where to start, where to end. I bet my grandmother is disappointed in me. I bet talking would be easier than sitting here, stiff and freezing. Just the thought of entertaining a conversation fills my brain with helium. For now, I simply eat Kiss after Kiss, pretending they're hers, and push the foils under the door, wondering what she does with all the empty kisses I give her.

GABRIEL CARLE (b. San Juan, 1993) is a writer and academic researching queerness, race, migration, and the environment in Caribbean literatures and cultures. They completed a BA in Escritura Creativa at the University of Puerto Rico, Río Piedras, and an MFA in Creative Writing in Spanish at New York University. They are based in New York City.

HEATHER HOUDE is a self-taught visual artist, writer, and translator from Philadelphia. She is the author of *Thin Skinned*, and her stories and translations have appeared in *A Gathering of the Tribes*, *The Common*, *Latin American Literature Today*, and the *Southwest Review*.

More Translated Literature
from the Feminist Press

La Bastarda by Trifonia Melibea Obono,
translated by Lawrence Schimel

**Blood Feast: The Complete
Short Stories of Malika Moustadraf**
translated by Alice Guthrie

**Grieving: Dispatches from a
Wounded Country**
by Cristina Rivera Garza,
translated by Sarah Booker

Happy Stories, Mostly
by Norman Erikson Pasaribu,
translated by Tiffany Tsao

Human Sacrifices by María Fernanda Ampuero,
translated by Frances Riddle

In Case of Emergency by Mahsa Mohebali,
translated by Mariam Rahmani

Panics by Barbara Molinard,
translated by Emma Ramadan

The Singularity by Balsam Karam,
translated by Saskia Vogel

Tongueless by Lau Yee-Wa,
translated by Jennifer Feeley

Violets by Kyung-Sook Shin,
translated by Anton Hur

The Feminist Press publishes books that ignite movements and social transformation. Celebrating our legacy, we lift up insurgent and marginalized voices from around the world to build a more just future.

See our complete list of books at
feministpress.org